seven day fiancé

a Love and Games novel

RACHEL
HARRIS

Entangled Publishing, LLC
2614 South Timberline Road
Suite 109
Fort Collins, CO 80525
Visit our website at www.entangledpublishing.com.

Bliss is an imprint of Entangled Publishing, LLC. For more information on our titles, visit http://www.entangledpublishing.com/category/bliss

Edited by Stacy Cantor Abrams
Cover design by Heather Howland

Manufactured in the United States of America

First Edition October 2013

Bliss

For the people of Carencro, Louisiana, who inspired so much of this story, and my beautiful tour guide (and cousin) Chantel. You are a blessing. Also for my husband, Gregg, whose unwavering love and encouragement proves that happily ever after truly does exist.

Chapter One

Shivering as cool November air kissed her exposed skin, Angelle Prejean quickened her pace across the Magnolia Springs Banquet Hall parking lot. The rhythmic *click* of her toe-pinching heels sounded amplified in the dark, but it did jack squat to drown out her mama's voice still ringing in her ears. What Angelle needed was a distraction, and an event planned by her crazy roommate was sure to deliver. Digging through her beaded black handbag, Angie fished out her ticket and flashed it at the entrance, then stepped inside the toasty warm lobby with a hopeful smile. It promptly froze and withered on her face.

What the…?

Looming directly across from her in the crowded vestibule stood an almost life-size poster of three faceless, shirtless men. The words FOR YOUR HOLIDAY PLEASURE were written in elegant swirling letters along the bottom.

For her *stupefaction* was more like it.

Angie glanced at her ticket, confirming she had the date and location right, and promptly returned her gaze to the glorious sight before her. Her breath escaped in a rush. Heat crept up her neck. But a herd of wild horses couldn't tear her gaze away. And from the excited whirr of murmurs and giggles filling the entryway, she wasn't the only one enjoying the man-tastic view.

Together, the half-nude beefcake trio in the poster was devastating, each man impossibly gorgeous. But for Angelle it was one man in particular, the one in the center, who had butterflies doing the cha-cha in her belly and her limbs gushing with warmth.

Cane.

It didn't matter that the image stopped at his throat. She didn't need to see his face to recognize the rugged bartender. The confidence in the man's stance, the ink on his skin, and the way her entire body shook with desire *and* trepidation gave his identity away. Thanks to the class they took together at Northshore Combatives, Angie had seen Cane Robicheaux in various stages of undress. But despite the overwhelming temptation, she'd never allowed herself the luxury of a thorough examination. In fact, she did everything she could to avoid eye contact of any kind—not an easy feat in a town as small as Magnolia Springs. Or with an attraction as fierce as hers. But now, alone with a bazillion other women doing the same, Angie let her eyes drink their fill.

Her gaze caressed the width of his broad shoulders. Traced the lines of his flat, rippled abdomen. And feasted on the artwork adorning his skin. A koi fish swam up one side of his smooth ribs, flames licked up a thick, muscular arm, and a cross with angel wings and his mom's name peeked from inside the other. An intricate yin-yang of a tiger and dragon covered the left side of his bulging chest, and she knew from prior, covert inspection that a fleur de lis marked his toned calf. The sound of her erratic pulse eclipsed all other sound in the room, but if Angelle were a betting woman, she'd put even money that a hum of feminine swooning was breaking around her. Cane Robicheaux exuded sex—sex and danger. And in spite of her many, many, *many* attempts to pretend otherwise, she was every bit as susceptible to that potent combination as the rest of the female population.

"Which is why I'm in so much trouble," she whispered with a disgusted snort.

A long shadow fell over the trio, breaking Angelle's lust-dazed trance. She blinked and shifted her attention to a statuesque brunette wearing a bright red evening gown and an amused smirk. "Sure puts you in the holiday spirit, doesn't it?"

"Uh, yeah." Angelle averted her gaze back to the poster as the heat of a blush extended to her cheeks. "That it does."

The annual Bachelor Auction was the town's official kick-off to the holidays and *usually* involved tuxedo-clad gentlemen and endless glasses of champagne. Of course, that was before her roommate and Cane's spunky youngest sister, Sherry, took control of the reins.

The brunette tapped a painted nail over Cane's chest. "Makes me want to do a little early Christmas shopping."

Irrational jealousy flared in Angelle's stomach. *Cane's not really mine,* she reminded herself. *Despite what my parents may think. This chick's free to bid on him if she wants.* But as the woman's lips tipped up in a cougar-like grin, that irrational flare grew into a blazing inferno of possession.

Chuckling to herself, the woman glanced at the elevated stage and catwalk centered in the room. "Good luck in there tonight. And may the auction gods be in *both* our favors, huh?"

Angelle nodded, forcing a brittle smile as the brunette sauntered away, hips swaying beneath the skin-tight fabric of her dress. Then, exhaling a frustrated breath, she began scouting for the bar. Normally, Angie wasn't much of a drinker, but if Cane was a bachelor up for bid—which she should've assumed considering he was *Cane*, after all—then she was gonna need the mental fuzziness. Otherwise, she'd likely do something to embarrass herself.

Such as win the man and then ask him for an *incredibly* crazy favor.

Looking past the image of forbidden flesh, her eyes slid over the long silent auction table boasting lingerie, jewelry, and highly questionable novelty items. Lining the floor beyond that were cramped cocktail tables decorated with what appeared to be *whips* and bright feather boas. A jolly, holiday-appropriate, yet completely incongruous Christmas tree was off in the far corner, holding ornaments she was sure would shock the country out of her if they were visible. To say Angie was out of her comfort zone would be an understatement of massive proportions. She was so far outside the zone she may as well be in a different zip code.

Why on earth had she thought an event by Sherry Robicheaux would be tame?

This was what Angelle got for not asking questions. She'd been too slammed between working shifts at the stables and volunteering at the firehouse to push for details, and her roommate hadn't exactly been forthcoming. Now she understood why. Sherry knew Angelle wasn't brazen like the brunette or a flirty vixen like herself. Nope, she turned five freaking shades of red simply ogling a damn poster.

Shaking her head with a grunt, Angelle turned to leave, her well-worn flannel pajamas and the Hallmark channel calling her name…and locked eyes with Colby.

So much for her escape plan.

Colby was Angelle's former rival turned friend. She was also Sherry's sister, and together the two women had taken her under their wings, practically making her an honorary Robicheaux. Now that Colby had spotted her, there was no way Angelle could get out of staying. At least not without admitting her considerably *non*-sisterly feelings for big brother Cane. Which she'd never do. The two women would be like dogs with a bone if they ever caught wind of her feelings—matchmaking, plotting, and hankering for a love match. She loved her friends to death, but despite her town newbie status, there was one thing Angelle knew as well as any native…

Commitment, in Cane Robicheaux's eyes, was a four-letter word.

Colby waved her over with a wide smile, indicating the empty chairs at her reserved table. A table located dead center facing the catwalk, giving them front-row seats to the debauchery beginning any minute.

Oh goodie.

"This is for charity," she reminded herself, propelling her feet forward. Her continued presence and the tightness in her belly had *nothing* to do with Cane being a bachelor. Or the fantasy of bidding on him. Nope, even her overactive imagination knew that was never gonna happen.

Audacious she wasn't. But oh, how she wished she were.

When she'd left her small hometown of Bon Terre, Angelle had vowed to reinvent herself. To leave the timid mouse behind in Cajun country, honor her sister's memory, and carve her *own* destiny for once. But nine months later, Angelle was still Angelle, just in a different town.

Her plans for taking on the big bad city of New Orleans had changed the moment she stumbled upon sleepy, sheltered Magnolia Springs. A suburb a mere thirty miles shy of her intended destination and a town that, while certainly different, was only marginally larger than the one she'd fled.

Her wish to be daring *did* lead her to become a local volunteer firefighter, a dream she'd held since she was nine years old. But it also only took three months of flinching at

every creak of the floorboard and whistle of the wind to kiss
her dream of living alone good-bye and move into a cramped
apartment with Sherry.

And finally—and perhaps the most distressing—it was
Angelle's overwhelming desire for more than a string of
Cracklin Queen titles and a life of inactivity that had landed
her in the biggest pickle of her existence.

The reminder of her ginormous lie, followed by the crazy
promise she'd made her mama just an hour ago made her
groan aloud. *At least when I make a mess, I make sure it's a
good one.*

Angie cut to the right as Colby lifted two glasses high
in the air. Either her friend was double-fisting for the night
or she'd miraculously read Angelle's mind. She hastened
her steps, the bright red drink calling to her like a beacon—
then pitched forward abruptly when her heel snagged on the
carpet.

Without thinking, she snapped her arms out to stop her
momentum.

And *whacked* an elderly woman upside the head with her
purse.

Time stopped. Then it fast-forwarded as Angie's eyes
widened in dawning horror. Wincing, she raised her head
and saw Colby sitting a mere two table-lengths away,
mouth twitching with laugher. Sadly, it wasn't twitching with
surprise, because this sort of thing was par for the course and,
unfortunately, how Angie rolled: ungraceful and clumsy, with
an added dash of socially awkward.

Bracing herself, Angelle turned to the poor blindsided
woman, who smiled as warmly as she'd expected, because
that was how residents of her new hometown rolled: forever
kind and forgiving, even when randomly assaulted. "Oh, Mrs.
Thibodeaux, I'm *so*, so sorry." She smoothed her hands along
the beaded sleeves of the elderly salon owner's gown, wishing

the ground would swallow her whole. "I didn't see you. I didn't—"

The gray-haired woman *tsk*ed, brushing her hands away. "Girl, that carpet's older than me, which means it's older than dirt. Your pretty shoes getting caught ain't your fault." She palmed Angelle's flushed face and gave it a not-so-gentle tap. "Now stop all this fussing over an old broad and go grab yourself a drink. It's almost time to win you a gentleman."

Angelle placed a hand over the woman's wrinkled one, grateful for the understanding. Of course, there wasn't a chance in Hades she'd win anything—or *anyone*. But that drink was sounding better and better.

After escorting Mrs. Thibodeaux to her table of friends, Angie finally made it to Colby's table. With a poorly disguised chuckle, her friend held out a tall glass. "You look as though you could use this."

"What gave me away?" she asked, making grabby hands for the drink. "My elegant stroll across the room or my cheeks flushing as red as my hair at your sister's welcome poster?" She took a long pull off the straw and made a yummy noise of contentment—*hurricanes, nectar of the gods*.

Colby laughed. "And here I thought that rosy flush was my brother's doing." Angie squirmed in her seat, and her friend winked knowingly. "As for the poster, I admit the majority of Sherry's schemes are questionable at best, but in this case I think she's onto something. Adding the Best Abs contest almost doubled advance ticket sales. Higher attendance means more money for Project Nicholas."

Angelle nodded, agreeing that anything that made more money for the local charity, which provided a Christmas for kids who didn't expect one, was indeed awesome. But then the rest of Colby's words sank in, and she choked on her drink.

Colby patted her back as Angelle slapped her chest. "Did you just say *Best Abs*?"

That explained the poster in the entryway.

Colby sat back with a frown. "Sherry didn't tell you anything about tonight, did she?"

She shook her head as lovely air made its way back through her windpipe. "That would be a gigantic nope. And I'm beginning to think that was intentional."

"You're probably right about that." A chorus of hoots erupted from the table behind them and Colby rolled her eyes, leaning in. "Well then, let's get you up to speed. The Best Abs contest kicks off the night. Instead of tuxes, I'm guessing the guys will be strutting around shirtless—most likely in Santa hats, if I know my sister. We'll vote for the bachelor with the most delicious six-pack, and then it's on to bidding on them like cattle." She grinned as she looked at the rock on her finger. "Well, *I* won't be bidding. But the rest of you will."

An image of a shirtless Cane in living hot color leapt into her mind, and Angelle's tummy fluttered. "I'm not bidding, either." Colby wrinkled her nose, and she clarified. "I'm making a donation, but I'm only here to support the guys Sherry roped into this thing."

Colby shot her a look of disbelief, but a woman with purple-streaked hair and a bright red getup a la Mrs. Claus chose that precise moment to walk out onstage. Angelle watched as Sherry surveyed the amassed crowd with a wide, maniacal grin, then waved enthusiastically when she spotted the two of them front and center.

"That girl has no shame," Angelle muttered. She pointed her finger with narrowed eyes, indicating her feelings on being bamboozled into coming, but Sherry merely sent her a dramatic air-kiss and Angie couldn't help but laugh. It was dang near impossible to stay annoyed at her quirky friend.

"Absolutely none," Colby agreed. "But to her credit, she offered to make tonight equal opportunity and let the women take part. Fortunately, no one thought Best Boobs on an event poster for charity would go over too well." They shared a look and broke into laughter. Only Sherry would suggest something like that with the genuine intention of being fair.

Magnolia Springs may not be the adventure Angelle had set out to find, but she was ever grateful for the detour.

Women began taking their seats, alerting Angie that the auction was about to begin. Her heart beat a strange rhythm against her breastbone and, removing her straw, she tipped her glass back and drained the remaining contents with one big gulp.

Colby gave the empty glass a pointed look. "So you're really not bidding tonight? Not even on an overbearing, good-hearted, bartender-slash-restaurant-owner?"

"*Especially* not on him," she answered emphatically, even as a voice whispered that doing so would solve her problem. Realizing that may sound harsh to the man's sister, she explained, "Not that there's anything wrong with Cane. Your brother's great. He's just not my type."

Colby snorted. Judging by that and the arch of her perfectly defined eyebrow, the talented chef wasn't buying the disinterested line of bull at all. Unfortunately, Colby had eagle eyes. She'd witnessed enough of Angelle's squeaks, blushes, and stutters whenever Cane flashed his dimples or showed her extra attention that she could call her bluff. But Angie planned on pleading the fifth to the grave.

The truth was that other than a passing, embarrassing interest in Jason (the fire captain who was now Colby's fiancé), Cane was the only man in town who'd even sparked Angie's interest. And he put the miniscule flicker of attraction she'd once felt for Jason to shame. That's probably because it hadn't even been *Jason* Angie had wanted. More like the idea of him. Her ill-advised crush had been back at the start of the summer, when her parents had first started hounding her.

Before her lies had snowballed. And she became short

one fake fiancé.

"Then sweetie, enlighten me," Colby said, resting her chin on her hand. "What *is* your type? Because as long as we've been friends, I don't think you've gone on a single date."

Angelle blew out a breath as she flagged a passing waitress with her empty glass. It was always fun when *that* depressing truth made its way into a conversation. "To be honest, I don't know," she admitted. "I haven't been on a first date since I was seventeen." Colby's jaw gaped, and she shrugged. "I didn't really date much before then, either. Brady, my ex, was a family friend, and we actually dated until right before I came here."

Right after he proposed in front of God and everyone.

Angelle wasn't proud of how it had gone down, or that she'd broken her best friend's heart. But they hadn't been right for each other. He had proved that by proposing so publicly, both embarrassing *and* forcing her to decline in front of all their loved ones. But they'd had no passion, no excitement. And other than having to tell him no in front of a packed auditorium, she had no regrets.

Shifting her gaze to her wrist, she touched the word she'd branded over her old childhood scar the very next day when she'd decided to leave home. It was a reminder of what she was searching for, what she was hoping to find, and now that she'd gotten herself into such a crazy scrape, perhaps even a suggestion on how she could get herself out of it.

Chance.

• • •

How in the hell do I get talked into this shit?

Taking in his reflection in the men's room mirror, Cane Robicheaux wondered if perhaps he'd lost his mind. Sherry had pulled some crazy stunts in the past, but this went beyond, even for her. He prided himself on always being there for his sisters, helping them with anything they asked. But after tonight, maybe it was about time he started telling them *no*.

The bathroom door opened, letting in the high-pitched squeals from the main room. *Awesome*. Just what he wanted—inebriated, horny, most likely middle-aged-and-over women. Never mind that was normal barfly material. At least when he tended bar he wasn't dressed like a male stripper. A familiar face appeared in the mirror behind him, mouth pinched in a pathetic attempt to contain a laugh as he said, "Ho-ho-ho."

Cane flipped Jason off, but it only made him laugh harder. "Your ass should be doing this shit with me," he muttered, slapping the damn Santa hat on his head.

His best friend for more than thirty years leaned his shoulder against the doorjamb and grinned. "Ah, but see, a perk of being engaged is getting out of the annoying crap your future sister-in-law asks of you." Cane narrowed his eyes, and Jason punched him on the shoulder. "Having a smoking-hot fiancée doesn't suck, either."

Cane grunted. Five months together and it was still awkward as hell hearing Jason call his little sister *hot*. And whenever Colby went there, Cane straight-up tuned her out. He had no problems with their relationship—marriage wasn't for him, but if they were happy, he was happy. He just didn't want to hear the gory details.

The door opened again, and this time his youngest sister stuck her head into the room. "Five minutes, Santa-man."

Jason tugged a strand of her dyed-purple hair. "Sherry, you realize this is the men's room, right?"

"Please," she scoffed. "Ain't nothing I haven't seen before. Besides, have you gotten a look at the hotties in this group? If I 'accidently' caught a peek at their bits, I certainly wouldn't cry."

Cane grimaced, and Sherry flashed him a grin, flicking the

white puffball dangling off the side of his face. He plucked the hat off his head and raked his fingers through his hair. "You owe me for this."

"Brother of mine, tell me, how is this different than any other weekend at the restaurant?" she asked. "You know good and well women line up the moment you step behind the bar, all on the off chance you'll shoot those magical dimples at them, and we rake in the profits. The only difference tonight is you're being ogled for charity."

Cane didn't give a shit about being ogled; Sherry was right, women did it all the time, and if admitting that made him a dick, so be it. But prancing around like a jackass wasn't his thing. Auction organizers had hounded him for years to be involved and he'd declined them every time. But when his baby sister did the asking… Of course, she'd waited until after he'd reluctantly agreed to mention he'd be a *shirtless* jackass, in bright red drawstring pants and a Santa hat.

He shook his head in disgust at his reflection. He looked like a damn pansy.

"Oh, cheer up, you grump," Sherry teased. "Buzz on the street is you're gonna raise Project Nicholas a crap-ton of money." Pushing up on her toes, she kissed his cheek, wiped her thumb over the red lipstick mark, and grinned. "Besides, it'll be fun. I promise."

Fun was a Friday night behind the bar. It was strumming his guitar after a long-ass day, grabbing a beer with Jason, or even watching a stupid teen movie with his godchild because it made Emma smile. It was balancing the restaurant's budget because he was screwed up in the head and enjoyed that kind of thing. He doubted any part of tonight would be *fun.*

As if playing devil's advocate, his mind brought forth the image of a jittery woman with haunting green eyes and a killer body. Now if *she* were in the audience, it would be a different story.

Sherry sent him another dazzling smile. "I'm off to gather the rest of the cattle—I mean guys. See your cute bootie out there." She blew him a kiss as she backed out the door, letting in another wave of horny female buzzing.

Jason chuckled under his breath, and Cane turned with a scowl. "Why are you here again?"

"To help Sherry with the sound equipment," he replied, unfazed. Grabbing Cane's hat from the sink, he held it out with a smirk. "Besides, you didn't think I'd miss seeing this, did you?" The gleam in his eyes promised he'd never let Cane live this down.

Yanking on the damn hat, Cane strode from the men's room. The line of half-naked bachelors extended down the hall, and with a shake of his head, he took his place at the back. Together they looked like a deranged elf's wet dream. Or a Christmas card for *Playgirl*. Jason slid him another smirk on his way to the sound equipment, confirming they looked as stupid as he felt, and a minute later, Michael Buble's "Holly Jolly Christmas" faded.

It was show time.

"What's up, Magnolia Springs?"

The response to Sherry's animated question was a wave of *whoop*s, and Cane rolled his eyes.

"Do I have a treat in store for y'all!" his sister continued. "Sixteen of the hottest guys in the area are here tonight: musicians, business owners, and local heroes, all eager to become your l-*ove* slaves."

The audience exploded again and Cane muttered, "I'm eager to get the hell out of this outfit." The guy in front of him turned and gave a nod of agreement.

"First up is the highly anticipated Best Abs contest!" Sherry shouted, and Cane could picture her gleeful smile. "One at a time, the men will strut their stuff on the stage, and it's your job to clap, squeal, and stomp your feet for the bachelor with the most toe-tingling, tummy-twirling, sinfully sexy washboard abs. And ladies, I got a sneak peek at the goods backstage and let's just say I know the temperature's cool outside, but it's about to get *hot* up in here!"

Another round of girlish cheers went up as the very *un-*holiday beginning of Right Said Fred's "I'm Too Sexy" rolled through the speakers. In unison, the line of guys' heads in front of him drooped. If he weren't so pissed, Cane would've laughed. Apparently, he wasn't the only one dreading this.

It just went to show how formidable his little sister's powers of persuasion were.

"Our first bachelor, Michael LeBlanc, is the newest member of the Magnolia Springs Police Department…"

As Sherry called out names and read each guy's stats, she'd pause for the women to show their approval. The whole thing was ridiculous. The dude in front of him took the stage, and Cane lifted his eyes to the clock mounted on the wall. Seven fifteen. In forty-five minutes, the auction should be over. Less than an hour of torture, doing his time with whomever *won* him, and then he could change back into normal clothes and get the hell out.

"Last but obviously not least, we have my brother, Cane Robicheaux. He manages Robicheaux's, the best Cajun restaurant not only on the north shore, but in the entire New Orleans area, in my ever-so-humble opinion."

At his sister's corny joke, the crowd laughed and Cane exhaled. Here went nothing. He stepped out from behind the curtain and the previous wall of laughter morphed into one of sharp whistles and innuendos. A woman in red near the front licked her lips.

Cane averted his eyes to Sherry, conveying again how much she owed him for this, then began walking across the long stage, eyes focused on the wall ahead.

"As most of you know, you can also find Cane behind

the bar on the weekends serving up your favorite drinks, and if you're lucky, you may just catch him on our small stage serenading the masses with his soulful voice and guitar. Cane's thirty-three years old, six-foot-two, and the three words he'd use to best describe himself are *tenacious*, *ambitious*, and *focused*."

Cane swung his head around, and Sherry shrugged.

She hadn't asked him any questions.

"The three things he can't live without," she continued, "are his family, his guitar, and Colby's beignets. His biggest pet peeve is dishonesty. And his idea of the perfect first date involves a bottle of wine, a quiet dinner, good music, and a *great* good-night kiss."

Up until that last part, he'd actually been impressed. As Cane turned to walk back across the stage, he mumbled for her ears only, "Better get used to the morning shift, little sister."

The agreement had been that she'd take all the opening shifts for the next two weeks in exchange for Cane doing the auction. After that little stunt, she'd extended her sentence to a month.

Sherry grinned. "As my big beast of a brother takes his mark, let's hear who thinks Cane Robicheaux has the Best Abs of the night!"

The applause was deafening. Before he knew what was happening, his sister had placed a bright red sash over his head, declaring him King of Abs. And he'd thought he looked like a pansy before.

Cane grasped Sherry's elbow, ready to inform her she was on permanent opening duty, when he lowered his gaze to the crowd and spotted *her* front and center. The one woman he wouldn't mind shouting innuendos at him. And the only one, other than his sisters, who currently wasn't.

Angelle's head lifted from her drink as if she could feel his stare. The spark of attraction she always tried to hide flared within her deep-set, vibrant green eyes—eyes Cane couldn't forget. He'd first seen them five months ago, shortly after the sexy redhead tripped over her own two feet and then apologized. He'd been hooked ever since.

Angelle was a mystery, as exotic and foreign as her French-sounding name. Guileless wide eyes, an aura of innocence, a voice like whiskey, and the word *Chance* inked on her wrist, she was the first woman ever to get under Cane's skin…and the first and only to appear ready to hurl whenever she saw him. Strangely enough, it only made him want her more.

Women didn't tell Cane no. If anything, they acted like the vapid red dress in the front.

But Angelle was too close. Near the danger zone. She was friends with his sisters, worked with Jason, and gave riding lessons to Emma. She ate at the kitchen table he shared with Colby more often than he did, which *should* make her off limits. Yet against every instinct and belief he had, Cane wanted her.

For months, he'd fought it. Tried ignoring the attraction, tried losing himself in other women. But in each face he looked into, he saw *her* eyes. Eyes so open and honest they gave all her thoughts away. Heard her sexy, roughened tone instead of the soft, feminine voices that used to turn him on. Nothing he'd done had gotten her out of his system, and he was starting to think the only thing that *would* was the woman herself. He needed to satisfy his curiosity for her and get his carefree, no attachment, no commitment life back on track where it belonged. Thanks to his father's infidelity, Cane wasn't made for forever—but he was good for one hell of a night.

And now was as good a time as any to prove that.

Usually, women chased him, but for Angelle Prejean, Cane was happy to play the hunter. He actually looked forward to it. Settling his determined gaze on hers, his lips tipped up into a smile as a slow flush rose in her cheeks.

Chapter Two

Holy molasses. The heat in Cane's stare could melt Angelle's panties. And the way it made her twitch in her seat, she almost wondered if it had. Never had a look of such intensity been directed at her before—not by the man in question, and certainly not by her ex. Brady had been many things, but *passionate* hadn't been one of them. She'd lost track of the nights she had spent lying in bed, fantasizing about what it would feel like to experience *real* desire. To be on the receiving end of such a burning look, knowing *she'd* been the one to inspire it.

Now that she knew, Angie could declare with all certainty that passion scared the ever-loving crap out of her.

Cane was a flirt. Not to mention a man-whore who was charming to boot. From the tattoos covering his skin to the cuts and bruises he often sported courtesy of the gym to the unruly and sexy-as-hell hair, the man was simply out of her league. And way, way, *way* over her head. Sure, he'd let her know he was interested, and she'd vowed to take more chances in her life—but not *that* much of one. There was taking chances and then there was duct taping her heart to a target and loading Cupid with the equivalent of a turbo missile. She wouldn't have a prayer's chance of recovering from a round with someone like him.

But that didn't stop you from putting your gigantic foot in your mouth, now did it?

Cringing, Angelle broke eye contact with the embodiment of sex—and the answer to her sticky engagement predicament—and ran headlong into his sister's smirk.

"But Cane's not your type, right?"

Knowing full well Colby had caught her undressing the man with her eyes—well, what was left to undress; seriously, he was practically naked up there—Angie chose to remain quiet. Colby covered her mouth with a delicate hand, which did absolutely nothing to hide her snort of laughter, and said, "Oh my, this is going to be fun."

"Happy to amuse you as always," Angelle muttered. She redirected her attention to Sherry, who was surprisingly announcing the first bachelor as sold for one hundred dollars. She hadn't even realized the auction had begun. Such was the power of Cane Robicheaux. The first bachelor, a cute kid who barely looked twenty-one, walked down the steps and joined his middle-aged winner, who promptly wrapped him up in her generous arms and did a happy shimmy.

Yep, I'm out of my element here.

Breathing through the heated stare she could still feel on her skin and the deep desire she had to meet it, Angelle picked up her drink and chugged.

The next half hour or so passed in much the same way, which was to say a blur of skin, sexy stares, exciting shivers, and her trying her best to ignore it all. With each new name Sherry called, the line of bachelors dwindled. And with each drop of alcohol consumed, the room's collective purse strings loosened. The winning bids grew. Several of the guys from the firehouse raked in more than two hundred dollars each, and with three empty hurricane glasses to her name, Angelle could even admit she was having a good time. Lovely warmth buzzed in her veins, a fascinating sensation since she rarely drank more than a glass or two at one time. Sherry was cracking her up with her antics and over-the-top commentary, the bachelors were laidback (and let's face it, yummy eye candy), and the winning women were hilariously enthusiastic. Angie was having *such* a good time, in fact, that she almost lost track of the lineup.

But when the second-to-last bachelor placed his Santa Hat on old Mrs. Thibodeaux's head and bowed to kiss her weathered cheek, every hair on Angie's body stood on end.

Cane was next.

Of its own accord, her slightly blurred gaze snapped to the stage, not surprised to find his already locked on her. A tingle ran down her arms, one that had nothing to do with the alcohol. Reaching for her freshly refilled glass, she held his gaze as she took another long, tart sip, and listened to the sound of her heart pounding in her ears.

"And last, but certainly not least, our very own King of Abs!"

At Sherry's gleeful giggle, Cane shook his head and closed his eyes. With their contact broken, Angelle stole a breath.

The entire room surged with energy. Energy and *hormones*. Women bounced in their seats. Purses opened. Tongues lolled. Sherry scanned the eager crowd and grinned as she said, "Let's say we start the bidding for our final bachelor at—"

"Two hundred and fifty dollars!"

A few tables over, the woman in red from earlier thrust a wad of cash in the air, and Sherry's eyes bulged. Every other bachelor had begun with a respectable bid of fifty dollars—but it appeared the brunette had come to play. Play and win.

Resentment roiled in Angelle's gut.

"All right, then," Sherry said, elbowing her brother in the ribs. "I told this man he'd be a money maker. So, our *opening* bid is two hundred and fifty dollars. Anyone want to take it to two seventy-five?"

Conversations broke out among the tables. Cash was counted, cell phones pulled out, and then a voice exclaimed, "Three hundred!"

Angelle turned to the willowy blonde who'd just appeared behind her. She was dressed in a festive green gown that left very little to the imagination. Diamonds draped her neck and hung from her ears, but her eyes flashed brighter than the bling. The woman looked haughty. She looked determined. She looked…not quite right. Her eyes were wide—almost wild—and they were fixated on Cane in a way that went beyond focus and into straight-up territorial.

After only a moment's hesitation, the brunette sprang into action, upping her bid to three twenty-five, and thus began a bidding war. Excitement and mayhem ensued. Angelle tossed back the rest of her drink. Her skin prickled, her legs twitched, and when she glanced down, the nails of her left hand had embedded into the soft leather of her purse. It must be the hurricanes because otherwise her reaction made no sense. Any time the two of them ended up alone together, she'd always pushed Cane away. She knew he was no good for her. But the thought of watching him walk off into the sunset with another woman made her stomach turn.

Especially if he walked off with the vixen in red.

Or the crazy-eyed chica in green.

When the latest bid upped it to four hundred, Colby made a low noise and stabbed her drink with her straw. Angelle quirked an eyebrow. And here she'd thought *her* reaction was baffling. Then she caught the weird look Colby exchanged with her brother and asked, "Okay, what am I missing?"

Colby lifted her chin toward the blonde. "That's Becca. An ex with Daddy's money to burn and a scary obsession with my brother. She stalks the restaurant, shows up at his shows. Apparently, they went out a couple times last year, but Cane said that was enough to know the girl was total Looney Tunes. He broke it off, but home-girl refuses to get the memo." Colby wriggled her shoulders. "I'm telling ya, Angie, the chick gives me the heebie-jeebies. You remember that woman in *Fatal Attraction*?" Angelle nodded and Colby pointed at the woman creeping closer toward the stage. "Glenn Close has nothing on Becca."

As if on cue, the blonde cried, "Eight hundred!"

A loud gasp pierced the air. At Colby's nod of agreement, Angelle realized the sound came from her own throat, but seriously, the woman *was* nuts. Becca had just doubled the bid—a bid *she'd* made.

The brunette gaped, blinked, and then frantically began digging through her purse. Becca cackled in triumph.

Swinging her gaze back to Cane, Angelle noticed him send their table a pleading look.

Colby lifted empty hands. "Sorry," she mouthed before turning to Angelle. "With the wedding in a few months, I can't be throwing around that kind of money." She checked her purse anyway, her lips pressing into a thin line. "No one in this town can. And Becca *knows* it."

Angelle bit her lip. See, that wasn't exactly true. What Cane's creepy stalker *didn't* know—what no one in Magnolia Springs knew—was that Angelle had money. Family money. Her grandparents had it in sugarcane, her parents had it in rice fields, but Angie's bank account was padded. Padded beyond what she made at the stables and fire station, and padded enough to rival whatever Becca thought she had. Angie just never went around flaunting it. She drove a used pick-up truck, shopped sales, and lived in her worn-out cowboy boots.

It was how she was raised. Where she came from, money in the bank meant you had security, but it didn't define you. It didn't change the person you were.

But in times like this, it sure did come in handy.

The brunette dejectedly lifted her head from her emptied purse. She shook it, and for the first time that night, Sherry's smile dimmed.

A loud *clap* rent the air as Becca began walking toward the stage to claim her *prize*, and the resentment in Angelle's stomach morphed into red-hot anger.

"Uh, going once," Sherry said slowly, dragging out the words.

Well, I did plan to donate to Project Nicholas anyway...

Sherry sent her brother an apologetic glance and called out, "Going...twice."

And if I do this, Cane will owe me...

Angelle rocked in her seat, knowing this could be the answer to her fiancé problem. She watched Sherry anxiously meet every eye in the crowd then hold a silent conversation with her sister. Colby lifted a slender shoulder as Becca reached the bottom of the stairs, cash in hand. Angelle squinted, positive she could see devil horns sprouting on the woman's head.

Displeasure radiated off Cane in waves as he shifted on his feet and raised his eyes to hers. Angelle's heart went out to him. This was bigger than her anxiety. Bigger even than her pickle. He needed help, and she was in a position to give it.

Sherry heaved a sigh into the microphone, the joy that had poured from her all night replaced with regret as she said, "If there are no other takers..." She paused to give the room a final hopeful glance, then squeezed Cane's enormous bicep. "Sol—"

Angelle clamored to her feet. "Fifteen hundred dollars!"

• • •

"Holy crap monkeys."

Sherry's response echoed through the quiet room. Cane wanted to laugh, but she made an excellent point. One more second and Becca would've won. And if she had, no amount of morning shifts would've made up for it. It wasn't that Becca was dangerous; she was certifiable. From the moment she'd shouted her bid, he'd been planning his escape. If he had to, he'd been prepared to cover the donation to Project Nicholas himself. But then his green-eyed temptress had come through.

Why?

Not even an hour ago, Cane had vowed to satisfy his curiosity with Angelle and move on, and here she was, handing herself over on a silver platter. After months of dodging him, turning tail whenever they were alone, spending the entire auction evading eye contact, she had saved him. He'd like to think it was jealousy—jealousy or attraction, he'd take either—but more than likely it was pity. No doubt, Colby filled her in on all things Becca. Add that to the unsubtle SOS vibes he'd sent her way, and the sweet woman couldn't help herself.

Guilt punched him in the chest. Followed by a softer emotion he chose to ignore.

As far as Cane knew, Angelle wasn't rolling in dough. She was a volunteer firefighter and taught horseback riding lessons to kids part-time for shit's sake. How in the hell did she have that kind of money to throw around?

Did she have that kind of money to throw around?

Sherry snapped out of her daze and quickly exclaimed before Becca could counter the bid, "And the King of Abs is sold to Angelle Prejean for fifteen *freaking* hundred dollars! Hot damn, Mama needs a drink."

The silent room exploded. Chairs screeched, glasses

clanked, and voices erupted. Angelle blinked, obviously shell-shocked, as women crowded her small table. She reached a blind hand to grasp the back of her seat and slowly sank down onto its cushion.

"What in the *hell* just happened?" Becca stood at the end of the stairs gaping, her eyebrows scrunched in the lost way he was ashamed to admit he'd once found attractive. That was before he realized that clueless was her usual look—other than the times she looked like a demon straight from hell—and he'd wised up.

Averting his eyes to his woman—damn, the thought of Angelle as finally being his for the night sent a jolt straight to his pants—Cane hopped off the stage to claim her.

He'd only taken a step when the psycho latched on to his arm. "*I* was supposed to win you."

Cane gritted his teeth in frustration. If he told Becca that it wouldn't have mattered, that they were never getting back together and that she needed to move on, he'd only be wasting his breath. She'd heard it all before; she just had selective hearing. Becca saw him as some sort of challenge, the one that got away. He'd been clear from the start that he wasn't looking for a relationship, back when she'd claimed she wanted the same.

When he was younger he'd always planned to settle down one day, but that was before his parents taught him what a crap investment relationships were. Feeling too much, getting too close to one person, meant getting hurt—or hurting someone else. Cane wanted no part of that, which was why he needed Angelle out of his head once and for all. But first, he had to get past Becca, and from experience, Cane knew responding to reason wasn't her thing.

"Yeah, sorry about that," he said, twisting out of her grasp and refusing to meet her intense stare. He stepped back and added, "But hey, happy holidays," before turning away, leaving her behind him.

I'm never doing this crap again, he thought, catching the furrowed line between Colby's eyes as he approached their table. She appeared as confused by tonight's turn of events as he was.

As for Angelle, she no longer looked dazed. She looked *lit*. She was face-first in yet another drink, and from his vigilant watch during the auction, Cane knew she'd consumed three hurricanes prior to this one. Four hurricanes, depending on their strength, were enough to knock some men on their asses—and this woman was tiny. Cane made a quick adjustment to his plans. He wanted Angelle in his bed, but he wanted her sober, consensual, and preferably well rested. But as she set down her half-drained drink and cautiously looked him in the eyes, he discovered one upshot to her current condition: inebriated Angelle didn't hide.

"Ho-ho-ho," he said with a smirk, watching a pink stain sweep Angelle's cheeks. "Having fun, ladies?"

Perfect white teeth bit into a full bottom lip as a small, sleepy grin softened her already angelic face. Overwhelming needs to both ravish and protect her hit him at once. The opposing reactions he got around Angelle were unsettling, but far from new.

Colby sighed and answered, "It's been a night of surprises, that's for sure."

Angelle nodded. Wrapping a long strand of auburn hair around her index finger, her gaze dipped to his bare chest. Her eyes gave a slow blink. "King of Abs," she drawled, reading his sash, her roughened, whiskey tone as sexy as ever, before turning to Colby. "Does that make you Sister of Abs?"

Colby laughed and slid Angelle's glass to the other side of the table. "That would be a no."

"What would be a no?" Jason asked, slapping Cane's shoulder on his way behind Colby's chair. He slipped his arms around his fiancée's neck and pressed a quick kiss against her lips. Then he asked Angelle, "That the size of Cane's sizable ego shrank after that cat fight?" He grinned to show he was joking, then caught sight of his co-worker's obvious condition and frowned. "You all right there, Ang? You look a little wasted."

Angelle waved a hand in the air. "Nah, I only had a couple—"

"You had four," Colby interrupted.

That seemed to surprise her. "*Four,* really?" But at both Colby's and Cane's nods of confirmation, she kept on trucking. "Perhaps I'm a bit buzzed, but it's all good."

Watching that lazy, sexy smile cross her face was indeed *all good,* and it gave Cane his perfect opening. "How about I drive you home, just in case?"

And there was the wide-eyed panic he was used to inspiring. "No. No, no, no. That's not necessary."

He leaned his forearm on the table, biting back a grin when he saw her fidget at his proximity. "Oh, but I think it is," he replied. *And not just for the safety of our citizens.*

"We could bring you home," Colby offered, her lips twitching at Cane's scowl. "Or you could wait for Sherry, since you're heading to the same place, but since she's in charge tonight, I have a feeling she'll be a while."

Angelle looked at her half-empty drink, tilted her head, and closed one eye. Then she nodded. She pulled the drink closer and wrapped her pink lips around the straw.

Cane had never been so jealous of a straw in his life.

Jason cleared his throat and Cane lifted his gaze. His friend chuckled as the opening notes of Etta James's "At Last" began to play. "I'm gonna dance with my fiancée for this song," he said, taking Colby's hand and helping her up. "Ang, meet you at the door when it's over?"

Angelle nodded again, and then they were alone. Cane

watched her sip her drink, strangely amused as her eyes focused on the crowd, the table, her straw, briefly his eyes, and finally his chest again. Obviously, if they were going to discuss the elephant in the room, he'd have to be the one to bring it up.

"So, our date," he said, grinning as she gasped around the straw and pushed away the glass. "Any idea what you want to do?"

She licked her bottom lip, then dragged her teeth across the plump skin as she ran her hands along the sides of her lap. Her eyes widened and then narrowed as her mouth opened and closed. She had *something* in mind, all right. But then she shook her head and attacked her drink again.

Interesting.

She lifted her head a long sip later, eyes sparking like she was committing some sort of internal dare. "Will you be at Robicheaux's tomorrow? I'd like to come by and proposition you."

Holy hell.

Now it was Cane's turn to widen his eyes.

Angelle slapped her hand over her mouth and sputtered. "*Shit,* that's not what I meant." It was a tossup what was funnier: hearing her sweet voice issue a curse or watching her wince and flail her arms. "I meant to say I have a proposition *for* you. Not that I want to *proposition* you. Not that there's anything wrong with you, but I just don't—you know. I mean, you're probably used to being propositioned. Happens all the time, right?" Then she screwed her eyes shut and stage-whispered under her breath, "Oh my God! Shut *up,* Angelle."

She was adorable. The flush on her cheeks, the uncomfortable squirming. Cane knew he shouldn't, but he couldn't help himself. Resting his other arm on the table, he pressed close and said in a low voice, "Just so we're clear"—he placed his hands on hers—"you can proposition me *any* time, angel." Her eyes shot open, and he grinned. "But yeah, I'll be at the restaurant tomorrow."

For one long moment, they stayed like that. Eye to eye, her sweet labored breath fanning across his chin. Close enough that if he wanted to press his luck, he could lean in and steal a kiss from those lips. But Angelle was like the skittish horses she loved so much. He couldn't rush her. This was a marathon, not a sprint, and he was confident she'd be worth the pursuit. So he settled for staring into her haunting eyes. They drew him in every time. One look and he knew everything she was thinking, everything she was feeling.

And tonight Cane saw confusion, fear, and—his absolute favorite—*desire*.

As the long, drawn-out words of "At Last" signaled the end of the song, Angelle lowered her gaze to the table. She grabbed her purse and slid off the chair, wobbling the moment her feet hit the floor.

Cane cupped her elbow to help steady her on her heels, smiling at her soft gasp. He lowered his mouth to her ear and said, "See you tomorrow."

He heard her squeak and then watched her walk away. But for the first time since he'd met the feisty redhead, Cane knew she'd be back.

Chapter Three

Hangovers were inventions of the devil. Angelle was convinced of it. They were punishment for drinking in excess, and in her case, trying to ignore the *un*ignorable—namely her giant pickle. And as if sluggishness and a migraine from hell weren't enough, thanks to last night's unwise inebriation, she'd also landed herself in an even bigger scrape than the one she'd been trying to forget.

If it were possible for faux pas to be an art form, Angie was an *artiste*.

Sweat pricked her forehead as she parked her trusty pickup in front of Robicheaux's. It was midday, and as Sherry had promised, the lot was deserted. Angie released a relieved breath. She still didn't have the foggiest idea how to explain the disaster she'd made or why she so desperately needed Cane's help, not to mention how he'd react to the whole thing. The fewer witnesses they had for this humiliating conversation, the better.

Angelle frowned as she pocketed her keys. Why on God's green earth did she drink last night? She was enough of a hot mess as it was without adding to it. She needed her brain fully functional to stand toe-to-toe with Cane, not wrung out from getting epically sloshed. But since she'd already poured this batch of lemonade, the only thing left to do was drink it. So Angie faked a sunny, confident smile, winced as even that small movement hurt her head, and hiked up the restaurant steps. Closing her hand around the doorknob, she inhaled a deep breath and then let it out as she tugged it open. Here went nothing.

Bells *ding*ed overhead as she walked inside and she flinched as the sound reverberated through her skull.

"Jumpy there, sweetheart?"

Angie's tummy fluttered, and for once this morning, it wasn't from nausea. She shifted her eyes toward the sinfully rich voice and felt the world drop out beneath her.

It should be illegal to look that good.

Cane's dark brown eyes danced with amusement as he folded his thick, muscular arms against the gleaming mahogany bar top. The soft cotton of his black T-shirt stretched across his broad torso and wicked flames peeked from the edge of his sleeve. Call her a victim of the classic bad-boy syndrome, but just thinking of the artwork left hidden gave Angelle the baffling urge to trace the designs with her tongue.

Before Mr. Tall, Dark, and Dangerous walked into her life, men with tattoos never held any appeal. If anything, they intimidated the snot out of her. Cane intimidated her, too, but it had absolutely nothing to do with the designs on his skin.

He made ink look *good*.

Cane cleared his throat, and Angelle realized she'd been gawking. Drooling a puddle onto the scuffed hardwood would be more accurate. Mortified, she averted her gaze to the back deck overlooking the bayou, wondering if a day would come that she'd be in the man's presence and not embarrass herself.

Angelle was used to being…less than poised. Awkward

Angie was one of her childhood nicknames, after all. But whenever Cane came within a half-mile radius, she left awkwardness in the dust. Her brain straight up short-circuited. A reaction that was not in the least helpful, since she hoped to be spending the rest of the week with the man. Alone. With no more hiding.

Rolling her shoulders back with renewed determination, Angelle forced herself to meet his eyes. "Is now an okay time to talk?"

The corners of Cane's mouth twitched. "Well, we *are* kinda slammed at the moment." He glanced at the one remaining straggler from the lunch shift and shrugged. "But I guess I can squeeze you in."

Two deep dimples appeared in his cheeks that, coupled with the low notes of his voice and the sexy wisp of ink peeking under his sleeve, turned Angelle's legs into cooked noodles. The man could make *anything* sound erotic… although it wasn't as if she had a ton of experience with that sort of thing. The one time she'd actually attempted to watch a porno, she'd been alone and way too embarrassed to finish it. And too concerned about what the camera crew was doing. Or if the men and women filming ever farted during a scene. But from her very limited knowledge, Cane would make a killing in the industry.

She rolled her eyes as she caught herself ogling his backside en route to their table. That was her—sweet, naïve, innocent Angelle Prejean, the only twenty-six-year-old in the history of forever sporting a chastity belt, trailing behind temptation incarnate. Hoping he'd agree to become her white knight in black leather.

Angie snorted as she pulled out a chair, and Cane inclined his head. "What's so funny?"

"Absolutely nothing," she said with an internal sigh. She shoved her hands through her thick auburn hair and laced them together on the table in front of her. Maybe if she stared at her chipped nail polish she could do this without sounding like a complete idiot. "So, last night—"

"You bid an obscene amount of money just to go out with me," Cane interrupted, his deep voice laced with humor. Her eyes shot to his and he winked. "You know, darlin', all you had to do was say the word. You could've had me for free anytime."

Sweet baby Jesus. Was she actually supposed to hold a thought in her head when he said stuff like that?

"Um, right." She cleared her throat, and his dimples deepened. "But I—I saved you from that lunatic, right?"

The naughty smile fell from Cane's mouth and he leaned back in his chair. "Becca." He bit out the name like a curse. "Yeah, angel, you did. And I appreciate it. That woman's a friggin' nightmare. But there's no way in hell I'm letting you go into hock for helping me." His brown eyes grew dark with determination. "I'm covering that donation to Project Nicholas."

Before he was even through speaking, she was shaking her head. The gesture was sweet, surprisingly so, but unnecessary. Angelle didn't need Cane to cover the bid. What she *needed* was for him to agree to her crazy scheme. But if the man felt as though he owed her, then that could only help her chances, right?

Willing forth confidence she didn't possess, she took a breath.

This was as good an opening as she was gonna get.

Angie lifted her palms to halt the argument she could already sense brewing. "Cane, you don't need to do that. I know I haven't talked much about where I'm from or my family situation, but trust me, I can handle the financial stuff. That's not a problem." She wet her lips and shifted in her seat. "I was glad to help you, honestly, and I didn't do it for any ulterior motives…"

She trailed off, simply unable to finish the rest of that statement. *Lord, why does this have to be so embarrassing?*

When she continued sitting there like the open-mouthed fish jumping in the bayou outside, Cane prompted, "But?"

But I need your help desperately, even though I'm terrified of what it'll mean.

That was the real doozy because while Angie needed Cane to get her out of this predicament, she knew if he did they'd be opening a whole other can of worms. It was like inviting Pandora to open a box of whoop-ass on her heart, her willpower, and her nonexistent love life. But she'd gone and made herself this mess. Now she had to live with the consequences.

Resigning herself to her ridiculous fate, Angelle closed her eyes and said, "*But,* I need you to be my fiancé."

. . .

Whatever *proposition* Cane had expected, it sure as shit hadn't been that. A few minutes ago, hell, a few *seconds* ago, he was confident he'd agree to anything that gorgeous mouth asked of him, as long as it didn't involve wearing a Santa hat. Apparently, he was wrong.

And apparently, Angelle was a little loco.

"You need me to be *what?*"

That familiar blush rose up Angelle's slender throat as her eyes popped back open. "Not for *real.* I need you to be my *pretend* fiancé," she clarified, like that somehow made so much more sense. She gnawed a plump lip and cringed. "I-I kinda got myself into a situation."

She seemed to sink into herself, and just like that, Cane's need to flee shifted into a need to protect. Worst-case scenarios began flashing through his mind. There was no doubt Angelle was tough. Volunteering at a fire station wasn't for the weak of heart, and neither was ninjitsu. In both endeavors, she stood toe-to-toe with the guys and fought as hard as any of them. That spunk was one of the sexiest things about her. But at the same time, Angelle was sweet, *too* sweet, and way too trusting. She'd be an easy mark for anyone wanting to take advantage.

Legs tensing, every muscle clamping down ready to take her and bolt, he asked, "Are you in some kind of trouble, sweetheart?"

Angelle scrubbed her hands over her face and gave a muffled snort. "Yeah, but not the kind you're thinking of." She waited a beat, then sighed, lowering her fists to stare gravely ahead. "This week is Thanksgiving."

Her tone implied it was a revelation, and Cane nodded, well aware of what month it was. "That usually comes at the end of November."

A spark of fire lit those eyes at his sarcasm. "Yeah, well, that's a huge holiday with my family. My dad's the mayor of our town, and every year we have a big festival and a parade. Almost everyone still lives in Bon Terre, most even on the same street, but a few of us have moved to larger cities. Thanksgiving is like our family reunion."

Cane didn't follow how this was a problem. Or what in the hell it had to do with her needing a pretend *fiancé*. Damn, the word alone acted like a vise on his lungs. Sucking in a breath he said, "That sounds…nice."

She rubbed her temples. "It normally is. But *normally* I'm not bringing home mythical fiancés." The smooth skin around her eyes tensed as she shoved a lock of hair behind her ear. "Mama called right before the auction yesterday. I haven't been home since I moved here, and she wanted to make sure I'm coming up for the week." She looked at him. "And that I'm bringing my fiancé so they can finally meet him."

Clearly, Cane was missing something. Growing up with

two sisters and a very verbose mom, he liked to think he'd become proficient in deciphering female speak—but Angie had him stumped. "Back up, sweetheart. I feel like I'm talking to Emma here. Why in the hell does your mom think you're engaged?" Angelle lowered her lashes. "And why can't you just tell her you're not?"

A frown tugged her lips and she began picking at the polish on her thumbnail. "I guess I better start from the beginning." Cane settled back in his chair. *That would be nice,* he thought, watching as she let out a long sigh. Pale pink polish flaked onto the tabletop. "Two days before I came to Magnolia Springs, my boyfriend proposed."

An unfamiliar surge of jealousy knocked him squarely in the chest. Cane had no claim on Angelle. He didn't want one. Love, relationships, marriage, the whole shebang was something he gave up long ago. But the thought of another man making Angelle his made Cane's blood boil. His hands tightened into fists in his lap.

"When Brady asked," she continued, oblivious, "it was like a wakeup call. If I said yes, I'd just be going from my parents' house to his. From one protected life to another, my future all planned out for me. I'm the baby of the family, and I've always done whatever people wanted. I even dated the man my parents picked, for crying out loud." She shook her head, the resolve on her face shocking—and hot as hell. "I couldn't do it anymore, Cane. I needed to live on *my* terms, you know? If that involved a man, great. If not, that was fine, too. Because it's what *I* would have chosen. My decision."

Angelle lifted her eyes and as usual, her every emotion swirled in their depths. Vulnerability, resolve, guilt, and fear. It was the fear that hit him the hardest. He covered her hand with his, and her lips parted in a gasp. Ignoring the electric jolt that shot up his arm, he said, "That couldn't have been easy."

"No," she said, swallowing hard. "It wasn't. Coming

here"—her small shoulders shook in a laugh—"that was *so* not a me thing to do. Mama flat out freaked, sure that I'd lost my ever-loving mind, and Daddy, he was fixin' to drive down here and get me. They kept hounding me on the phone to come back, harping on the 'good man' I left behind. I needed them to see that I'm fine here, you know? That I'm great. I have a job I'm proud of, an apartment I got without their help, and friends I love to death. The only thing I *don't* have here is a man." Angelle dropped her gaze again and shrugged. "So I made one up."

Cane didn't know if he should laugh or run. But neither would help him understand what the hell she'd been thinking. "And so you figured why bother dating when you could just pull a fake fiancé out of your ass?"

She winced, and immediately he felt like a jerk. Jokes and sarcasm were his family's go-to response, but as fierce as she could be, Angelle was delicate, too. He needed to remember that. "It wasn't like anyone real was beating down my door," she mumbled. "Cane, you know I'm shy. I don't exactly know a ton of men. But I never expected it to go this far. It started small, just one date, one little white lie to get them off my back. For weeks, it worked like a charm. Until it didn't. Then one date turned into many and before I knew it, Mama called fresh from a visit with my *perfect* ex and out popped my mythical man proposing."

Her shoulders slumped, like her outburst zapped every ounce of energy she had. It probably had, since it was the most the woman had ever said directly to him, other than a squeaked hello. She looked tired and lost, and an intense need to help her rose within him.

But one thing still didn't add up.

"Why me?" She squirmed at the question, and his curiosity piqued. "Trust me, I get meddlesome moms. When mine was alive, she expected grandbabies the second I graduated college, so I had to develop my own diversionary tactics. Not as farfetched as yours," he added with a teasing smile that got her to snort. "But if this has been going on for months, you must've dropped a name at some point. And it's no secret I'm not your favorite person."

The flush rose on her pale cheeks, and Cane remembered the crush she'd had when she first moved here. His jaw clenched in irritation. "Who did you say was your fiancé, angel?"

Eyes wide at his growly snarl, she yanked her hand away. He sat back, folding his arms tight across his chest. Of course she'd said Jason's name. Before he proposed to Colby, Angelle had followed him around like a lovesick puppy. *That's* the reason Cane was suddenly the perfect candidate for this job. She was coming to him not because of the intense attraction between them or because she knew she could trust him to help. She came because Jason was already a fiancé. Cane shook his head. If Angelle thought he'd pretend to be another man on top of this stupid engagement shit, she had another thing coming. Cane was through with looking like a jackass.

Not that he was really considering this ridiculous *proposal* anyway.

"You," she whispered.

The word was so soft, so low, that Cane almost didn't hear it through his inner tirade. When he did, his gaze shot to hers. "What did you say?"

Angelle cleared her throat. "At first, I *didn't* give them a name. They didn't ask—I think they were just too stunned— and I sure as heck wasn't giving them one. I was still shocked myself. But I knew they'd call back, so I went to find the only guy I really knew in Magnolia Springs. A man I knew my parents would adore. Someone safe, dependable, and solid. It was that night at Grits and Stuff, do you remember?"

Jealous fire burned his veins but he nodded. "The night

we met."

"Right." She wet her lips and looked back down. "I figured it was time I got out there again anyway, so I thought I'd kill two birds at once. Who knew, maybe it wouldn't have to be a lie for long. I came home thinking I'd made real progress. But when Mama called back later that night…I didn't give her Jason's name."

More surprising than what he now knew was coming was the sense of triumph it gave him. "You didn't?" Cane prompted, needing to hear Angelle say the words. It shouldn't matter to him, since he knew this couldn't go anywhere past a hot night or two in bed, if he was lucky enough for even that. But for some reason, he needed to know that first meeting affected her as much as it had him.

Angelle shook her head. Her green eyes filled with vulnerability as she said, "I said *your* name, Cane. My parents think *you're* my fiancé."

The swinging door to the kitchen fell open. Two wide-eyed faces peered around as Angelle let out a muted squeal. Cane wasn't surprised, though. His sisters eavesdropping had been a given; he was just shocked they hadn't busted their asses at the *first* fiancé bomb.

Fiancé.

Damn, it was like a plot from one of Sherry's soap operas. This kind of shit didn't happen outside Hollywood or those red-covered books he'd cleaned out of his mom's closet. Or, so he'd thought.

Cane couldn't deny a part of him was ready to jump at this. He wanted her, *needed* to get her out of his head, and she'd all but admitted his *non-safe* reputation was the reason she was so skittish. What better way to get Angelle to relax and topple her monumental defenses than spending a week alone, pretending she was his?

But there was another part of him—the side that protected

women like *her* from men like *him*—that knew this could be dangerous. He liked Angelle. He respected her. And the last thing he wanted was to see her hurt. A one-night stand or an extended no-strings-attached fling was one thing. But a week of faking real emotions? That was a whole other ball game.

The promise he'd made long ago burned brighter in his mind. Twelve years ago, he witnessed the devastation his mother went through and even though his parents eventually reconciled, Cane vowed he'd never let himself inflict that kind of misery.

He wasn't his father.

Movement behind Angelle's lowered head snagged his attention and Cane watched as his sisters exchanged a look. They turned to him with matching smirks, and he exhaled.

He knew that look. He was about to be ganged up on.

Sherry stepped forward, grinning widely. Ever the matchmaker, she was enjoying this and he knew it. "You already have a ring," she mentioned, oh so helpfully. "Mom left you hers, and you know what a romantic she was. She'd *love* it if you used her engagement ring to help Angie."

His more sensible sister hitched her hip on the neighboring table. Colby sent her friend an encouraging smile. "And we've got the restaurant covered. As much as my big brother likes to think otherwise, we'll survive a week without him quadruple-checking every aspect of this place." She grinned and blew him an air-kiss. "Love ya, bro. Besides, we're closed Thanksgiving, and Devon and Kara can handle the bar this weekend."

So much for practicality. Everything lined up. They'd taken any feasible excuse he could've had and chucked it right out the damn window. All three women turned to him with expectant faces, and Cane knew he was done for. Especially when Angelle's eyes softened with hope.

"I'll give you the ring back, of course…" she said, her voice breaking off into a whisper. "You know, when we come home." Her teeth sank back into that plump lower lip as she shifted in her seat. "I just need to get past this holiday, let them see I've moved on. After that, I'll start dropping hints about problems, and then be single again before Christmas."

Cane scrubbed a hand over his face and sighed. She'd done him a solid with Becca. Now it was his turn to help her. It wouldn't be completely altruistic; he fully intended to return with his curiosity satisfied and his obsession with the auburn-haired vixen sated. He'd just have to find a way to keep Angelle at a safe distance while doing it.

Even with the sense of dread roiling in his gut, an unmistakable surge of excitement rushed through his chest. He'd wanted to make her his for a short time. He'd just never thought it would happen quite like this. Taking her hand again, Cane linked their fingers together. They may as well get comfortable with the PDAs if they had a chance in hell of pulling this off. "So, when do we leave?"

Chapter Four

"Uncle Cane, you're getting *married*?"

Choking on his swig of Dr. Pepper, Cane bit back a curse not meant for a young girl's ears. This day just kept getting more bizarre. It had begun quietly, alone in the big house his parents had left him, with the same old monotony stretched before him, and somehow ended with him engaged. Not for real, of course, but evidently, that detail was insignificant. Tossing another pair of faded jeans on the stack of books in his open bag, Cane turned his head and feigned innocence. "What, sweetheart?"

"I overheard Dad and Colby talking downstairs," Emma explained, waltzing through the door and heading straight for his guitar. Colby split her time equally between their childhood home and Jason's, and her soon-to-be stepdaughter always followed in her wake. It was sweet how much she idolized Colby, how excited she was that they would all soon *officially* be a family. But as much as he loved spending time with his godchild, she could be exhausting. And rather nosy. "Personally, I think it's awesome. Angelle rocks. She's *so* much better than those hoochies you normally date."

There was so much wrong with that sentence Cane didn't know where to begin. Emma knowing about the other women, the word *hoochies* being a part of her vocabulary, her learning about this crazy scheme…any way he sliced it, the onslaught of horror was overwhelming. But unfortunately, she wasn't all that wrong about the other women.

"Bug, I think you heard wrong." Cane scratched the side of his stubbled jaw as Emma turned from strumming his guitar, lips tugging in a confused frown. Strangely enough—considering he'd agreed to this farce—he hated lying. He despised liars. But the whole truth was too ridiculous even for a twelve-year-old. So he said, "Angelle just needs help with a…situation. And I'm tagging along to do it. As friends. That's all."

His godchild's smile didn't dim in the least. In fact, it grew. And that made Cane nervous.

The entire Robicheaux/Landry family was infected with wedding fever. Bridal magazines were in the bathroom, diagrams of seating arrangements littered the dining table, and discussions about the growing RSVP list for Colby and Jason's wedding played on repeat—and now Cane was contributing to the insanity. The fact that this was all an absurd hoax didn't seem to faze either of his sisters. They'd begun planning the pretend event anyway.

Which was why he'd barricaded himself in his room, packing for the stupid trip. Normally, Cane didn't give two shits about what he wore. Or what people thought of it. As long as they weren't getting close, he was fine with whatever impression they got of him. But Angelle had his head all twisted. Was he supposed to be himself or dress to impress her folks? How far did this scam go?

Angelle had said they knew everything about him, that he managed Robicheaux's, tended bar on the weekend, rode a motorcycle, and played in a band. Other than leaving out his tats and highly coveted King of Abs title, she pretty much summed up his stats.

The ones he let the world know, that is.

Very few people knew about his OCD-like quirks, love for calculus and physics, addiction to Sudoku, or fascination with the Discovery channel. Or how at the age of twenty-one, the plans for his future altered. And the possibility of him getting married for real vanished.

It was rare someone got close enough to learn any of those things. Or for Cane to *want* anyone close enough so he or she could. As always, Angelle defied his normal logic. He already felt more physically drawn to her than any anyone he'd ever met, and he was attracted to the woman she let his friends and family know so well. From her comments earlier and general wariness around him, it was obvious she'd made assumptions based on what he let the world see. It was probably better for both of them if he let her keep them.

"Tell Angelle my signature colors are green and blue," Emma declared, snapping Cane's attention back to the present. He lifted his head to see her listing the rainbow on her fingers. "But I guess I can work with yellow or purple, too. Oh, it could be like an LSU wedding!" She jumped up and clapped her hands happily, then grew serious just as quickly. "But no taffeta bows on the butt, please. That mess doesn't work on anyone."

She rolled her eyes and then with a mischievous giggle, spun on her heel and skipped away.

Cane blinked. "Taffeta?" What in the hell was that, some kind of snack? Raising his voice he asked, "Colors?"

"Duh," answered her amused, disembodied voice from the hall. "For the bridesmaid dresses." Her tinkling laugh clearly said she was enjoying his distress. And that he could add one more wedding planner to the mix.

Great. Just what he needed—his highly impressionable, preteen niece playing Cupid.

Emma's matchmaking with Jason and Colby was already family legend. Between her and Sherry, his closed-off best friend and stubborn-as-hell sister hadn't stood a chance. But Angelle wasn't Colby. And Cane sure as hell wasn't Jason. The two of them weren't headed for a happily ever after. They were simply two highly attracted people, agreeing to *pretend* for the hometown busybodies, and then "breaking up" the moment they returned to town.

With Angelle officially cleansed from his system.

Cane's gaze drifted to the bed, imagining red hair splayed across his pillow. Getting the uptight woman to give in to their attraction wasn't going to be easy. But there was no doubt in his mind that Angelle would be worth the effort.

Grinning, he zipped up his bag.

• • •

Angelle was gonna puke. Her hands were so clammy her perfume bottle slipped from her grasp, and a swarm of horseflies was dancing the jitterbug in her tummy. Ever since she'd left Robicheaux's she'd been one big bundle of anxiety, and her completely addicted to love, *highly* enthusiastic roomie wasn't helping with that one bit.

"You realize at this moment we're practically sisters," Sherry said, riffling through Angie's dresser. What the woman was looking for was anyone's guess, but Angelle was certain it would end up being embarrassing. "Fake engagement or not, the chemistry between you and my big brother is explosive. You know y'all are gonna have to act all lovey-dovey to sell this thing, and I predict some *serious* fireworks occurring." She bumped the drawer closed with her hip and frowned. "I'm just pissed I won't be there to see it."

Ah, crap. Sherry was right. Pulling this off would require a lot of acting, and Angelle had the theatrical skills of a turnip. She and Cane had chemistry, all right—*crazy* chemistry—so the feigning starry-eyed passion in public didn't worry her. It was pretending she *wasn't* crazy about the sinfully sexy man when they were in private that would be the problem.

An image of Cane wrapping her up in his big, strong arms and plundering her mouth flashed in her mind, and Angie's tummy flipped again.

"And I predict it'll be a freaking miracle if anyone buys the charade," she said, sinking onto her bed in a defeated plop. "Sherry, what have I gotten myself into? Seriously, Cane and me as a couple? It's laughable. The two of us couldn't be more opposite."

"Exactly," Sherry declared with a smirk. "And opposites make for some yummy sparks." She wiggled her eyebrows and did a shoulder shimmy, then said, "Now you hang tight for a sec; there's something I want you to borrow for the trip."

As Sherry scooted out the door, Angelle pulled her knees up to her chest. Guilt and hopelessness made her head spin and with a sigh, she laid her cheek against soft, well-worn denim.

What she was asking of Cane was huge—but what she was asking of herself was even bigger. Her gaze flicked to her wrist, the word *Chance* taunting her. So far, her new life mission had a 30 percent success rate. In other words, she wasn't doing so hot. Cane represented the exact kind of guy she *should* be going after. Passion personified. Adventurous. A man totally different from her ex.

And yet, so similar to the man her sister had been dating when she died.

Angelle's wrist throbbed as pain and regret sliced through her. She wanted to be like Amber, to take risks and live life to the fullest. But was she following *too* closely in her sister's footsteps? Air hissed between her teeth as she imagined her daddy's reaction to Cane's ink. She'd left that detail out for a reason, wanting to delay the fallout.

Her forehead thunked against her knees. Maybe it wouldn't be as bad as she imagined. Cane was a business owner, after all. He was strong and handsome and, despite his womanizing ways, obviously a good man. He worked hard and his sisters doted on him, as did Emma.

Which meant her heart was in serious jeopardy. She frowned.

Maybe she *should* call things off now, before it was too late.

But then her thoughts turned to her mom and she sighed. Angelle had left her alone to deal with the town reaction to from her breakup, and it hadn't been pretty. Mama was so eager to show off her engaged daughter, excited she could finally put a positive spin on the story of her runaway bride–like daughter. Knowing her, she'd invited half the town to welcome them home, and Angie only needed one guess as to who'd be sitting front and center.

Groaning, Angelle closed her eyes. Brady would be there, all right, if for no other reason than to show he'd moved on. Since their very public breakup, they hadn't spoken. Not directly, at least. Mama made sure to fill Angie in on all things Brady during their daily conversations, and Angelle was sure her mom did the same with him. But now that she was home, there would be no avoiding him. Their families were old friends, and the town was small. And that, more than any other reason, was why she needed Cane by her side. Yeah, the man inspired forbidden fantasies that would make even wanton women like Sherry blush, but he was strong. When the wolves descended, and they definitely would, she could lean on him to get her through it. Maybe even tap into that well of cool, calm confidence he naturally exuded and take a little for herself.

She'd just have to be extra vigilant that in doing so, she didn't let herself believe the lie.

Strictly professional.

"All right, chica, I got ya a few options."

Angelle looked up to see Sherry reenter her bedroom, arms laden with a multitude of lace, silk, leather… Her eyes widened in shock.

"Sorry to tell you this, sweets, but your negligee selection is pitiful," Sherry declared with a shake of her head. "And that mess simply won't be tolerated as long as you share my apartment and have me as a friend. You're way too sexy to hide under cotton and flannel. When you get back we're totes hitting up Victoria's Secret, but for now, these will do."

An explosion of colorful unmentionables hit her bed, and blood rushed to Angelle's cheeks. She and Sherry were so not on the same page. Picking one up, she noticed two significantly placed cutouts on the bodice and dropped the garment as if it would bite her. "Ah, wow. Thanks for the offer, Sher. It's very…generous of you. But, um, this stuff *really* isn't me."

"That's kind of the point." Smiling, she sat down and shook Angie's knee. "Listen, I'm not trying to pimp out my brother. But the two of you are going away together for a week. I'd be failing in my job as your friend and sex-obsessed cheerleader if I didn't make sure you were prepared. Besides, can you honestly look me in the eyes and say you're not attracted to him?"

Angelle held her gaze for a nanosecond and then looked away, unable to lie. *See, zero acting skills.* Sherry plucked up another option from the pile, a green one with lace, and draped it over her knees. "This one looks amazing with your coloring."

Angelle banged her head twice on the soft fabric. Nine months living here, five of them spent as an honorary

Robicheaux, and all her secrets were tumbling out in one twenty-four-hour period.

"Sherry, I honestly don't think I'll be needing any of this stuff." She traced the scalloped lace trim with her fingertips, too self-conscious to look up as she admitted, "And the reason I *know* I won't be needing any of it—" She swallowed and buried her face in the silky fabric. "Is because I'm a virgin."

Silence.

Complete and utter silence.

I've actually shocked Sherry mute.

Up to this point, Angie hadn't thought that was possible.

When the waiting became unbearable, she lifted her head and found Sherry studying her in confusion. Forehead wrinkled, she said, "But you had a boyfriend." She tilted her head in wonder and gazed as if Angelle were the eighth wonder of the world...or something equally mind-blowing. "He proposed."

"Girls with boyfriends and even almost fiancés can be virgins, you know," Angie muttered, trying super hard not to feel offended or annoyed. Living with Sherry, conversations sprang up all the time where she could've volunteered this information and didn't, so this had to come as a shock. But the expression on her friend's face was exactly why she hadn't said anything before. "Look, at first I waited because I wanted to be in love. Then, even when I believed I was, it still never felt right. Brady assumed I wanted to be married first, but I don't think that was it."

Sherry nodded, her lips pursed slightly as if in thought. "I respect that. So, what, do you think you were just never really in love with your ex?"

Angelle shrugged. "I know I loved him as a person. I still do. He's a good guy and was a great friend to me. But honestly? No, I don't think I was *in* love with him. I think we became more like two friends who hung out and occasionally made out than a couple destined for an epic romance. There was no excitement, no passion. And I think that's what was missing. If I had those things, it wouldn't matter if I were married or not. I'm not sure it would even matter if I were in love. If it feels *right,* then I'll gladly join the ranks of the hymenally relieved, but until then, I refuse to settle for anything less than what I deserve, either."

A smile played across Sherry's mouth. "Damn, girl. I think I just fell in love with you a little bit."

A laugh exploded from Angie's throat. It wasn't easy being a secret virgin living with a self-proclaimed nympho, and admitting it aloud was like the weight of the world had been lifted from her shoulders. Angelle knew her V-card was nothing to be ashamed of, but it felt good to be accepted. And now that her friend knew the truth, she'd understand why her gift, while being extremely thoughtful, was completely unnecessary.

Winking, Sherry took the green nightie from Angelle's lap…and placed it in the opened suitcase. When Angie started to protest, she held up her hand. "I heard you, okay? I heard you, I respect you, and if I swung that way, I'd be going after you myself after that speech. But you and my brother? Major excitement. Off-the-charts passion. And blocking out the fact it *is* my brother in the other half of this equation, it pays to be prepared. If this is gonna be your first time, I want my girl looking *good*. Especially since I pay attention and know it's your birthday this weekend," she added with a grin. "Don't you want to give yourself a little treat?"

It *was* her birthday this week—a detail Angelle hadn't mentioned while propositioning Cane. Obviously, she had to tell him eventually. The last thing they needed was to get down to Bon Terre, have everyone buy their act, only to have it blow up when her own fiancé didn't know something as basic as her birthdate. But in a way, Angelle wished everyone would forget it. Being the center of attention had been hard for her even when she was young. She used to cry during the Happy Birthday song, until Amber suggested she picture everyone as SpongeBob. Then after she died, it became sad *and* uncomfortable.

Unaware of Angelle's inner turmoil, Sherry grabbed a string of silver packets from under the pile of garments and dropped those in her suitcase, too. She made a V with her fingers, pointed at her eyes, then Angelle's, and then pointed back to the case. "Again, prepared."

Angie shook her head with a smile. There was no arguing with Sherry, and it wasn't as if sexy lingerie and condoms would make any difference. A week alone with Cane wasn't magically going to make it easier to be around him or make her see him in a new light. He was still a player, still dangerous. Still temptation incarnate. Speaking of which… "Just, please don't tell your brother about this, okay?"

Sherry's jaw dropped. "Are you kidding? I'm lobbying for us to become sisters here. No offense, but the last thing I want to do is advertise you're uncharted territory. Cane has a hero complex. If he knew you were a virgin, he'd go all chivalrous. No, I'll let *you* drop that little bombshell yourself in the heat of passion."

The heat of passion. A shiver rolled down Angelle's spine as her overactive imagination fired up an image to match that description. Cane lowering himself over her, those brown eyes darkening to almost black. His mouth doing delicious, unspeakable things to her body. Her writhing under him.

Holy hot flash! Angie released a breath, fanning the air up in the hopes of cooling herself down. Sherry laughed and stuffed another outfit into her suitcase, this one black leather.

Cane Robicheaux was dangerous. If town gossip were to be believed, he had more experience than Hugh Hefner and would no doubt rock her innocent world. But he did bring the passion and excitement. Her gaze shifted to the remaining scrap of silk on the bed. Maybe giving in to their attraction—just a *little*…a few hot kisses, perhaps a bit of exploration—could be a good thing. She could check "experience real passion" off her to-do list and help the two of them appear more smitten for her hometown in the process. After all, engaged couples do make out. When her brother Troy got engaged, he and Eva could barely keep their hands off each other. Angelle would be a *couillon*—a complete idiot—if she didn't go into this week remembering that. Not to mention it'd be a giant red flag for her folks.

So, if Angie *did* decide to throw caution to the wind and take a chance—again, just a tiny, itty-bitty chance—it would be for the good of the ruse. Taking one for the team. For strictly professional purposes.

Angelle bit the corner of her lip and met Sherry's knowing gaze. "Give me the purple one, too." *Just in case.*

Chapter Five

Just over two hours. That's how long the trip from Magnolia Springs to Bon Terre was. Cane hated being still for two *minutes*, and sitting inside a truck for that long was practically torture. That's why he had bought his bike. Riding demanded his total attention, complete immersion. With the wind hitting his face, the energy of the engine ripping through his body, and his synapses firing to stay alert, Cane felt alive. Free. Unconstrained.

But damn if driving with Angelle tucked beside him, the sweet scent of sunflowers filling the cab, didn't make him feel alive, too. And turned on. This plan of his better work. So far, close proximity only served to heighten his desire, and it was beginning to grate on his nerves. Tightening his grip on the steering wheel, he asked, "Anything I should know before we get there?"

Angelle startled. Cane realized it'd been quiet, with not even the radio playing, for going on ten minutes. Apparently, they'd both been lost in their own thoughts. And from the way she'd jumped at the sound of his voice, he'd like to know what hers involved.

With a nervous laugh, Angelle glanced over, dropped her gaze to his mouth, and then quickly looked away. *Interesting.* "Well, yeah." Then she frowned. "A whole lot of stuff, actually. If you're my fiancé, you should probably know everything there is to know about me. And I should know about you, too."

The smooth skin between her eyes furrowed as she nibbled on her bottom lip—an expression Cane had seen far too often over the last five months. It meant she was worried, nervous, maybe even scared, and for once, he could understand why.

"Don't worry about it, angel. We'll figure it out." He sent her a confident smile, hoping he was right. Spending the holiday with this charade blowing up in his face was something he'd really rather avoid. "We have two-plus hours to get a crash course in each other. Plenty of time to hit the highlights."

Angelle nodded distractedly, clearly unconvinced, and began tapping a rhythm on her lap. Cane knew a thing or two about nervous habits, so he placed his hand over hers to calm her down—and caught her shiver from the corner of his eye. The tapping stopped, and he bit back a smile.

Now unable to help himself, knowing his touch affected her, Cane encircled the slender bones of her wrist with his thumb and finger. Angelle was tough, but she was also much more delicate than any woman he'd ever known. So feminine and vulnerable. The contradictory mix fascinated him. It brought out every protective instinct he had, and attracted him like nothing else before.

On the underside of her wrist, the site of her tattoo, he felt the raised skin of a scar. Curious if the injury linked to the mysterious one-word brand, he grazed the pad of his thumb over the mark. Her pink lips parted. When he did it again, her head lolled, and her breath caught.

The stuttered sound, the rise and fall of her chest, the way her hand flexed and curled as his thumb drew slow circles… it only made him want her more. He hadn't thought that was possible. And when her head shifted and she peered up at him with unmistakable, unhidden desire, well, it was all over.

Cane gunned the accelerator. Flipping on the turn signal, he switched lanes, headed for the rest stop an exit ahead. Angelle's voice was whisper soft when she asked, "Where are we going?"

"We need to get something out of the way right now."

In the quiet of the cab, he heard her swallow. There were no other words until he threw the truck into park a half mile up the road. As soon as he did, Cane chucked his seat belt, made quick work of hers, and stared into her unguarded eyes.

Angelle was one giant tell. If she ever tried playing poker, she'd lose her ass. Her family bought the fiancé lie up to this point because she hid behind a cell phone and several hundred miles, but the two of them wouldn't have that luxury this week. People would be watching them like hawks, curious about their relationship, looking for sparks. And luckily, they had *that* in spades.

Brushing a lock of auburn hair away from Angelle's face, Cane said, "This charade isn't going to be easy. I'll learn everything you want me to know, everything we have time for during the drive. But darlin', there's one thing we don't need to work on. And that's this."

He lowered his forehead to hers, feeling the soft pant of her quickened breath hit his opened lips. He skimmed his nose across hers and closed his eyes as he breathed deeply. Sunflowers. A hint of vanilla. Cherry-scented lip gloss. And Angelle. *His* Angelle, at least for the next week.

Angling his mouth so their lips were barely touching, he said, "Desire, Angie. Attraction. We have it. We don't have to fake that. And since we're alone, and that's *my* ring on your finger, it seems only fair I get to steal a kiss."

Anxiety mixed with excitement entered the emotional gumbo of her gaze, and her tongue flicked out to wet her lips. It brushed over the seam of his mouth, and he growled low in his throat. "Our first kiss of *many*."

Then, closing his eyes, pretending he didn't see the sudden flash of affection in hers, he dropped his mouth and kissed her.

He kissed the shit out of her.

That desire he'd said they had, well, it damn near set off an explosion in his truck. Fire, heat, panting breath. Thoughts that had no place in a cramped cab alongside a busy highway, at least not in the light of day. But hell if he wasn't wishing he'd stopped at a hotel instead.

Angelle was soft—soft hair, soft lips, soft sighs of pleasure. And she tasted sweet. So damn sweet. This was his bit of heaven, right here, and while Cane had no right to keep her long, now that Angelle was in his arms, he knew one night would never be enough. To get this woman out of his head, he'd have to extend his plan. It'd take at least a week with her in his own bed, stopping to refuel only when it became an absolute necessity. But he couldn't rush this. This was Angelle. She required an entirely different game plan than the women he was used to. She needed to be wooed.

So, with his lips and tongue, Cane began showing her exactly what he wanted to do to her body. Everything he *hoped* to do before the week was out. And when her tiny, tentative hands reached out to grip the fabric of his shirt, he grinned.

Cane tore himself away from her sweet lips to slide his tongue along the column of her neck. A gasp escaped Angelle's mouth. She was so responsive. She made him feel like everything was new for her, like he was the first man to make her feel like this. Pride and satisfaction coursed through his veins. He bit and then licked the underside of her jaw, and a deep moan broke free from her throat. And that released the hellcat.

Suddenly slapping his hands out of the way, Angelle knotted her fingers in his hair. Cane chuckled as she tugged roughly on the ends, impatiently yanking him closer and herself higher. Placing his hands around her slim waist, he slid across the seat and tugged her onto his lap. She settled a leg on either side of his hips and they shared a hiss.

"Good Lord." Her voice came out a slur, almost dazed, and only a sliver of green peeked from beneath her thick fringe of eyelashes. But it was enough to see she was as into what was happening as he was. "So *this* is what it feels like."

"What *what* feels like?" he asked, molding her curves with both hands. God, she was perfect. He had to keep reminding himself that their first time could not be at an overgrown rest stop on the side of the interstate in broad daylight.

Now, a motel room right off the interstate…

But as soon as that thought entered his mind, he felt it. A shift in the air. Angelle's loose limbs tensed. Her spine straightened and her eyes widened. Dropping her gaze to his chest, she answered, "Kissing the mighty Cane Robicheaux, of course."

Placing her hands on his shoulders, she pushed herself off his lap. Cane sat there a moment, stunned.

What just happened?

This woman ran fire hot and ice cold. He rubbed a hand over his face, trying like hell to catch up. And telling his libido to slow the hell down. Sliding his hand to the back of his neck, he squeezed the muscles and watched as she lowered the visor and began smoothing the lines of her smudged lipstick, the hellcat officially back in its cage. "Everything all right there, angel?"

"Peachy." Angelle fluffed her hair then snapped the visor

back in place, smiling at the windshield. Avoiding eye contact. "But we should be getting on our way. Knowing Mama, she has a huge spread prepared, and trust me, we don't want to be late."

Glancing at the clock, Cane figured she was right. By the time they got to Bon Terre, it'd be after one. He had a hunch showing up late wouldn't make the best impression—but he'd be damned if this truck was going *anywhere* until he got a good look at those eyes. He needed to see what in the hell was happening in that gorgeous head of hers before they budged an inch.

"I don't know," he drawled, stretching out his long legs as much as the cramped cab would allow. He leaned his head back and shrugged. "I thought we'd make a stop at the Harley store in Scott first. I'm starved and I hear they have a few good places to get cracklins around there, too. I was thinking we'd look around a bit."

Angelle's head whipped around so fast it would've been comical, had he not been preoccupied with the hidden secrets in her eyes. "Are you serious?"

"No," he answered, searching her face. Confusion faded, leaving behind wariness, embarrassment, guilt, and even a shade of desperation swirling in the green depths. Whatever made Angelle shut down a moment ago was big. Important to her. And it didn't have shit to do with her mama's planned lunch.

Cane wanted to pry. He wanted to make her tell him what had spooked her so badly. But he couldn't. Obviously, he'd pushed too far, made some mistake, and he didn't want to do it again. If he wanted Angelle comfortable around him, then he couldn't force her. She had to come to him, open up to him, on *her* terms.

Scooting back behind the wheel, he buckled up, knowing she was still watching him. He shot her a grin he didn't feel.

"Just messing with ya, sweetheart." She released a breath and settled back in her seat, reattaching her seat belt. Cane shifted into gear. Reversing from the spot that would be forever etched in his memory, he said, "Let's go meet the folks."

Cane kept Angelle distracted during the drive. He asked about her family, her childhood, her favorite subjects when she'd been in school, and the activities she'd liked. Unsurprisingly, horses topped the list. Riding, training, breeding, as long as it involved a horse, Angelle enjoyed it. What did shock him was learning she'd been a math and science nerd, too. Cane had her pegged as a quiet literature or maybe a history girl, but Angelle's face lit up discussing biology and physics. Discovering they shared an interest in the way the universe worked was refreshing and unexpected. And completely frustrating.

Cane didn't need another reason to feel connected to Angelle.

He liked her too damn much as it was.

More surprises came learning about her family's large chicken population, and that her closest sibling had been ten years older. He caught the past tense and wanted to ask, but he bit his tongue. He'd vowed to keep things light—for now. So instead, he asked about her hometown. Angelle's somber mood instantly lifted as she proceeded to give him an earful about Bon Terre. By the time he took the exit, Cane was sure he could lead the town tour.

Waiting at a stoplight off the busy interstate, Cane glanced around. "I can't tell you how many times I've driven past this exit, but I can honestly say I've never been here before."

Angelle laughed softly. "Not many people have. We're a small town, but we like it that way. Our annual festival and parade draws a decent crowd, enough to feed the local economy. But come Sunday evening, they head on out, and we're left again in peace."

Peace was an apt word. As he drove under the overpass, every lyric to every country song he'd ever heard came to life. Fields of crops, old dirt roads, and red pickup trucks. With the song "Mayberry" by Rascal Flatts playing in his head, Cane asked, "Anything else I should know in the next three minutes?"

She thought a moment. "Just be prepared to meet the welcome wagon. My family's big to begin with, and I guarantee at least half the town's population will be waiting on my doorstep. The prodigal child returning home is gossip enough, but they gotta be chomping at the bit to meet the *city boy* I tricked into marrying me."

Angelle labeling herself a prodigal child was humorous, but what he laughed at was, "*City* boy?" He shook his head. "Have any of these people even been to Magnolia Springs?"

"Doesn't matter," she said with a shrug. "Anyone who's not from the country is considered city. Around these parts, that normally means Lafayette, but in comparison to home, even good old Magnolia Springs is *city*."

Cane shook his head with a smile. He doubted it could be that much different from where he grew up. It appeared Bon Terre had more land and less traffic, but people were people. And with the last name Robicheaux, no one could say he wasn't Cajun. He glanced over and noticed Angelle's lips twitching with barely concealed amusement. "What?"

A full laugh broke free as she pointed to his Converse sneakers. He'd figured they would go over better than his motorcycle boots, but apparently, he'd guessed wrong. "You're gonna catch so much crap for those."

He rolled his eyes, returning the wave of a passing driver. It wasn't as if he owned any cowboy boots. And to be honest,

Cane didn't care if the whole damn town had a problem with his footwear, especially when it made her laugh like that. "So everyone will be waiting to meet the *city* boy who sports messed-up kicks. What else?"

Angelle fidgeted with her fingers and turned in her seat to face him. "There's a very good chance Brady will be leading the pack."

Cane kept his face purposefully neutral. The truth was he hoped she was right. He'd like to meet the idiot who let her slip through his fingers. "How long were you two together?"

Without hesitation, like it was no big deal, she answered, "Eight years."

He cursed and swiveled to look at her. "Eight *years*?" Angelle bit her lip and nodded, big green eyes saying he was failing to make her feel at ease… but *damn*. "And in all that time, he never tried to put a ring on your finger until this past year?"

"Well, for seven and a half of those years, we were apart. Different schools, different states…different wants," she added on a sigh. "After graduation, I hung around town, working at the library, helping my parents take care of the animals, waiting for Brady. He was so busy with med school it just didn't make sense to get married any earlier. And I wasn't ready to leave home. Bon Terre was all I knew. When Brady finally came home last Christmas to start his residency in Lafayette, it was the first time we'd lived in the same city since we were eighteen."

Anger churned inside and his fists clenched the wheel. "So basically, you put your life on hold for a part-time relationship with a man who put you second best. Is that what you're telling me?"

The guy held her on a string for years, and to hear her tell it, he came across as honorable, waiting until he finished school to give her a ring. In Cane's opinion, any man who asked a woman like Angelle to wait around twiddling her thumbs for eight years wasn't a man at all.

He glanced at *his* ring sitting on her pretty little finger and grinned. Fake engagement or not, he'd succeeded where her ex hadn't, and call him a jealous jackass, but Cane was eager for Brady to see that.

"It wasn't Brady's fault," Angelle said, twisting his mom's ring and admiring the heart-shaped diamond. "He did eventually propose… I think it was just too late. We'd both changed—at least I had. I couldn't spend another three years waiting for him to complete his residency, waiting for my own life to begin. But when I said no, Cane, I didn't only break Brady's heart. I broke the *town's* heart. That's what you have to know before we get there. Brady and I were Bon Terre's golden couple, the mayor's daughter and the high school quarterback turned 'good doctor.' That's what everyone calls him, by the way." She mumbled something under her breath he couldn't hear. "That's why I left. I couldn't start over here with the entire town disappointed in me. I needed a fresh start."

"Bon Terre's loss is Magnolia Springs's gain," Cane replied, turning onto a long two-lane road with fields on either side. "And I, for one, am glad you left."

He sensed her heavy gaze on him and turned to meet it. Her lips lifted in a smile. Not a timid or embarrassed one, not even a shy or inebriated one. Angelle smiled her first, full-fledged, authentic smile in his direction, and Cane's chest tightened. "So am I," she said.

They drove again in silence, and after another mile, the paved road turned to gravel. Angelle told him to turn down Papa P. Blvd. "That's my *papere*," she said, pride evident in her voice. "My grandfather," she explained. "But everyone just calls him Papa. This is our family's road."

Cane slowed to take in the sight. Acres of green land

stretched before them, some with cows, others with horses, and many with what appeared to be large fields sectioned off in between. Just from the small strip Cane could see ahead, Angelle's family road contained at least seven or eight homes, all similarly styled: comfortable, obviously Southern, with large sloped roofs and porch swings. Without tall buildings or even a ton of trees off the main road, the bright blue Louisiana sky seemed endless.

"That's my brother Troy's house on the right," Angelle said, pointing at a house with yellow siding. "My cousin Lacey lives on the left up there, next to my nanny and *parrain*." She sent him a wink. "That means godfather, city boy. My grandparents are all the way at the end, and that's Mama and Daddy where all the cars are."

Cane's eyes widened. It wasn't just where all the cars were. It appeared to be where the entire town was. Angelle hadn't been lying when she said they'd all come out for their appearance. Rows upon rows of trucks were parked along the street and in the nearby field, and people were everywhere. Crossing the street, standing in the grass, and for some reason, chilling in their cars talking with the windows down. A large crew was waiting on the front porch, gathered around a couple Cane assumed were Angelle's parents, sitting on…was that a *church* pew?

"Why is there a church pew on your parents' porch?" he asked, following the ever-so-helpful motions and points of practically everyone, directing him to a spot saved front and center. At least fifty pairs of eyes, if not more, were trained on them. Cane lifted a hand in a halfhearted wave.

Why did I agree to this again?

The reason why laughed beside him. "Uh, yeah. It was a gift from the priest when they remodeled the church." Angelle shrugged a shoulder and grinned. "Why? Doesn't everybody have a church pew on their front porch?"

"No. No, they don't," he replied.

"Well, welcome to Cajun town." She laughed again and jumped out of the truck. Leaning her tight body through the open door, she said, "Don't just sit there. Get on down."

Get on down. Where Cane was from, that meant busting a move on the dance floor. Angelle's wink and saucy grin implied she knew that, and that this was the first of many cultural shocks and confusions he'd experience over the next week. But anything that lit her up like that was fine by him.

With nothing to do but follow his amused redheaded tour guide into this *Cajun town*, Cane turned off the engine, pocketed his keys, and stepped onto the circular drive.

Chapter Six

Being home was like a shot of caffeine straight to Angelle's veins. She'd spent so much time worrying about the reaction she'd get when she arrived that she forgot how special Bon Terre really was. This town was a lazy Sunday tubing down Bayou Teche. It was a bowl of her grandmother's prize-winning gumbo and a link of her favorite crawfish *boudin*. It was driving down endless back roads to clear her head, wading through a crawfish pond checking traps, and watching Papa pray over her niece's sprained ankle. Life here was slower, the people were family, and the food…Angie inhaled deeply and grinned.

Cane may think he's Cajun, but Cajun country's gonna rock his world.

She glanced at her fiancé for the week. For all her stress about acting the part, she deserved a freaking Oscar for her performance during the ride. Pretending Cane's kiss hadn't knocked her silly or melted her into a puddle of goo on the floorboard of his truck had required skills Angie hadn't known she had. Forget about passion scaring the crap out of her or being utterly out of her league sexually. If *that* was what she'd been missing, then sign her up for more. A whole *lot* more. She wasn't breaking out the lingerie, and there was no way in Hades she was ready to do the nasty, but those kisses were mighty fine. As long as she kept that line between charade and emotion in place and her fool mouth from practically declaring her virginity in the process, she was good to go.

Cane caught her staring and sent a flirty wink. *Busted.*

Flinching, Angelle dropped her gaze, digging the scuffed toe of her cowboy boot into the soft grass, hoping with everything in her that he hadn't also read her thoughts.

"*Petite fille*, you gonna grin at the ground all day, or are ya gonna give your mama a kiss?"

Laughing, she raised her head and squinted into the sun. "Well, it *is* a pretty fine patch of ground." Her mother smiled as Angelle ambled across the driveway and made her way up the weathered steps. She leaned down to hug the woman's neck. "Hey, Mama."

Angie could be eighty years old with grandchildren of her own and the tiny dynamo holding court on the church pew would always be *Mama*. And the salt-and-pepper lovable grump beside her would always be Daddy. When she turned, he stood and pulled her into his strong, Old Spice–scented arms. Angie blinked back tears. Why had she stayed away for so long?

Reining in her emotions, knowing everyone was watching, she nodded toward the sea of faces scattered around the yard. "Did you declare my homecoming a town holiday? Because if not, I think some of your good people are playing hooky."

The beloved mayor puffed up his chest, but she caught the twinkle in his eyes. "Don't you talk about my constituents, *petite fille*. These good people missed you, yeah." He looked away and cleared his throat. "So have we."

Seeing the solid, stoic man get sentimental nearly broke

the dam on those tears she'd blinked back. "I missed you, too, Daddy."

They stared at each other for a long moment, him tight-lipped and nodding, her losing the war on her emotions. Luckily, a familiar voice cut in saying, "Little Red, ain't nobody was missing this show."

Angelle spun around with a squeal, causing her gathered aunts, uncles, and cousins to laugh as she raced forward. Lacey Sonnier, her blond-haired pixie other half, hopped off the porch railing. Growing up, they'd been thick as thieves, spying on their brothers, telling tales in the stables. Their marathon phone sessions grew less frequent after the first few months in Magnolia Springs, and a punch of regret hit Angie's chest for not keeping in better touch.

Wrapping her in an enthusiastic hug, Lacey twirled her around, plopped her back on the ground, and announced, "Our Cracklin Queen's returned!"

With only a slight wince—she was mostly used to her cousin's antics by now—Angelle rolled her eyes. "And ready to pass along the title," she muttered with a laugh. She had nothing against the honor, other than the requirement of eating her weight in fried pork fat. It just felt like one more tie to the *old* Angie. The girl she was trying so hard to leave behind.

Lacey grinned. "Honestly, Little Red, you didn't think you could sneak back and not stir up the phone tree, now did you? You're the hottest piece of gossip this town's seen in years, and *everybody* wants in on it." A heavy footfall came from the steps, and her blond eyebrows flew toward her hairline. The buzz of conversation around them ceased. "Especially when the gossip looks like *that*."

Angelle couldn't believe it. Just that fast, the enormous lie she'd told had slipped her mind. Memories of her and Lacey pranking their older brothers had swept her away so completely that she'd blanked on all the reasons she was here. This wasn't a simple family reunion. She was a woman on a mission. A mission to prove how *fabulous* she was doing on her own, and convince her hometown that quiet little Angie had somehow landed the sexy beast standing behind her.

Lacey muttered a string of naughty curses under her breath, utilizing the words *holy* and *hot* in ways that made Angelle blush. Or maybe that was the man himself. She turned to smile at her so-called betrothed, and her breath stuttered.

Holy boudin balls, is right.

There was no denying that Cane was scrumptious—and completely out of his element on her family's weather-beaten porch. There wasn't one thing that she could point to and say, *that's what targets him as a city boy.* It was everything put together.

It was just Cane.

From his sexy, disheveled hair (sans ball cap), to his stubbled jaw and lack of cowboy boots, Cane screamed city. Add in the trademark battered black leather jacket draped over his thick forearm, and you had the epitome of an outsider. Sure, his casual outfit was common enough, but the way Cane *wore* it made all the difference.

Dark wash jeans rode low on his trim hips. Black cotton hugged the defined muscles of his chest and arms. He held out a large, calloused hand, beckoning her closer, and a hint of a tattoo peeked from beneath the edge of his sleeve. Angelle's heart thudded.

Mine, she wanted to scream to the row of female cousins creeping closer, even as she darted a glance at her daddy, wondering if he'd spotted the ink. Instead, she swallowed past the lump of nerves lodged in her throat and placed her hand in his. "Everyone, I'd like you to meet Cane Robicheaux."

His mouth lifted in a slow, devastating grin as he tucked her into his side. A chorus of sharp inhales met the embrace.

And when the dimple popped in his left cheek, Angelle heard Lacey mutter, "Oh my."

Turning back to face her family, Angie added, "My fiancé." *Three, two, one…*

Feet hit the deck as her relatives surged forward. Wood creaked, metal clanked, shoes scuffed. Of course, they knew she was bringing him today, had been scoping him out since the moment they pulled onto the road, but she'd just given the green light for the inquisition.

Her oldest brother, Ryan, reached them first, but Troy and her daddy were right behind. Her *parrain*, three uncles, and five male cousins followed. All the women watched from afar, but from the looks in their eyes, Angelle knew they were every bit as curious.

Ryan folded his arms across his chest. He narrowed his eyes and lifted his chin, but the man beside her didn't flinch. Her police officer brother was strong, formidable, and seven years Cane's senior, but there was no beating her fake fiancé when it came to general bad-assery. After what seemed like a solid minute of silence, Ryan relaxed his stance a fraction, and with a glance at Angelle, held out his hand. "Welcome to the family."

Happiness and guilt warred in Angie's gut, but she joined the others in a sigh of relief as the two men shook hands. "Thanks for having me," Cane replied, and the sincerity in his voice tightened her stomach. For one brief moment, she let herself imagine what it would be like if this were *real*. Then Troy stepped forward, and Angelle whisked that unhelpful thought away.

Ryan may be the eldest, but Troy was the brother they needed to win over. They were the closest in age, and over the years, he and Brady had become friends. The two men had a lot in common, and they'd counted on being brothers one day. In fact, Angelle was surprised (although thankful) Brady wasn't standing beside him right now. He must be waiting with the others in the backyard. But Troy's friendship with her ex, coupled with his need since childhood—especially since Amber died—to stand as Angelle's protector, made her extremely nervous. She loved her brother. Respected his opinion. And under normal circumstances, his approval would mean everything, along with her daddy's. But this wasn't normal. It wasn't *real*. Knowing that didn't make the situation any easier, however. It added a whole new dimension.

Observant eyes flicked to the wisp of ink on Cane's bicep. His sleeve had risen while he'd shaken Ryan's hand, and wariness edged with disapproval radiated from Troy's tense shoulders. Angelle shifted to hide her so-called betrothed's arm behind her and silently pleaded, *Please, just let me get through this first meeting with minimal drama.*

Troy's brow furrowed as if he'd read her thoughts. He probably had, because his own were clear as day on his face—they'd be discussing this later.

Turning back to Cane, he said aloud, "Troy Prejean." Reaching back, he snagged his wife's hand. "And this is my wife, Eva."

As the tall blonde stepped forward, Angie held her breath. The rest of the porch seemed to follow suit. This was it. The moment her brother would or would not give his approval. Troy's thin lips pressed together and then he said, "Good to meet you."

Angelle flinched.

Anywhere else in the world and Troy's greeting probably would've been fine. But in the south, in Cajun country, in *this* situation, that was as close to fighting words as a welcome got. The renewed rigidity of Cane's spine said he noticed. And he wasn't the only one.

After Troy, her *parrain* was up next, followed by her cousins and uncles, each man welcoming Cane and issuing similar statements of cool acceptance. It was unclear whether this was in solidarity to Brady or protecting their Little Red against the big bad city boy. But either way, she and Cane had an uphill climb ahead, and Angelle had no one to blame but herself. By always keeping to the background, following the path others laid out for her, she became the girl everyone looked out for, took care of, and protected. While she appreciated their love, she was now a grown woman. She could make her own choices.

Eventually, all the men fell back. And only Daddy and Papa remained.

Cane glanced at Angelle as the older men stood there, nodding stiffly. It was the first time she'd ever seen the Magnolia Springs playboy nervous. He had a right to be. Troy may prove difficult to win over, but her *papere* was the patriarch of the family. And the only true path to her family's acceptance would have to come from her daddy.

And honestly, Angie couldn't tell *what* was going on in the man's head.

He and Brady's dad were close—the mayor and the chief of police. They were old friends who'd expected to become in-laws. Then there were the unmistakable similarities between Cane and her sister's ex. But Angelle wasn't Amber. She wasn't a teenage girl rebelling against her parents. She was an adult bringing home the man she loved—er, that she wanted her daddy to *believe* she loved.

Now those dang horseflies were back, dancing the two-step in her belly. She may be a woman, but she was still a "good girl" at heart, and the thought of disappointing her father twisted her insides. Cane squeezed her side as if he could sense her anxiety, and her daddy's eyes widened a fraction. Lifting his gaze from Cane's large hand around Angelle's waist, Daddy looked at Angelle and then at the amassed crowd. Music floated on the wind but the porch was silent, waiting. Cane's grip tightened.

The familiar mayoral smile slid into place as her daddy stepped forward and slapped Cane on the shoulder. "Hope you're ready to eat, son."

Cane's slightly forced grin returned. "Always, sir."

• • •

Angelle's childhood home reminded Cane of his own. Stained wood, family collages, and crucifixes. Potted plants lined the windowsill, colorful magnets decorated the refrigerator, and warm rugs covered the floor. She'd implied she came from money, but nothing about this house screamed wealth. It was simple, laidback, and well-kept. And it made Cane like the Prejean clan even more. He understood their lukewarm welcome. It made things slightly more difficult, but he admired her brothers in particular for their protectiveness. If Sherry brought home a stranger who looked like him, Cane would be cautious, too. Setting his bag down in what appeared to be Ryan's former room, he scanned the trophies staggered on the bookshelf and released a breath. The show was on.

After he got the old man's shoulder slap, Angelle's mom had led them back here. She'd kindly, but *pointedly*, explained that they'd be maintaining separate rooms while under her roof, then smiled and offered him a cold drink. Although the sleeping arrangements weren't conducive to his plans, Cane couldn't help but smile. The sweet and sassy woman reminded him of his own mother, and he missed her like crazy.

A family picture on the nightstand snagged Cane's attention. A mud-splattered Ryan sporting a UL Lafayette uniform and holding a football dominated the frame. His smile was wide and carefree—but that's not what drew Cane's eye. It was the scrawny redhead perched on his shoulders. Strolling over, Cane picked up the photo with a smile. Angelle couldn't be more than five or six years old.

On Ryan's right stood a teenage Troy with his arms extended in the air, his face full of acne. On his left, with one hand on Angelle's knee and the other flipping off the camera, was a young girl with dyed-black hair and heavy makeup. Even with the gunk, it was obvious she was a Prejean. Her smirk was teasing, her eyes full of laughter, and the love in Angelle's eyes as she watched her was unmistakable. This was Angelle's sister. A sibling Cane hadn't yet met. And if he had to guess, the sibling that *had been* ten years older.

Cane studied the family dynamic for a few more moments, curious about their history. Wondering if he'd ever find out. He didn't know Angelle well, but he'd become somewhat of an expert on reading pain. There were ghosts tied to the memories of her sister. Secrets that, if he was right, had changed his favorite redhead…something Cane knew a thing or two about. For now, he wouldn't push her for details or answers. He'd keep it light and carefree. But he would keep watch.

With a final glance at Angelle's gap-toothed smile, he returned the photo and then followed the sound of her sultry, whiskey voice down the hall.

"Thank the Lord Mama didn't ask to help me unpack," Cane heard Angelle say as he neared her opened door. "I'd have sent her to an early grave."

Nudging the door wider, he glanced around the room, noticing the frilly lace, collection of stuffed animals, and the fact that she was alone. Cane grinned. "Knock, knock."

Angelle startled, a fist of purple silk clutched near her heart. Her fair cheeks flushed as she followed his gaze and she quickly spun around, shoving it deep within her suitcase.

So Angelle had packed lingerie for the week. That was promising.

He leaned a shoulder against the doorframe, smiling.

"Were you just talking to yourself, sweetheart? I have to say that rosy glow has me wishing I'd kept quiet a little longer. Seems I might've liked what I overheard."

Scowling, she shoved her hand through a section of thick auburn hair. "Nonsense. Despite what the women of Magnolia Springs have caused you to believe, not *every* thought or conversation revolves around the almighty Cane, you know."

"I never said it did, darlin'," he replied with a wink. Her cheeks burned a touch brighter. Call it a hunch, but Cane had a feeling the lady protested too much. And with her making it a point not to look anywhere near his general direction, he figured that was a good thing.

She bit her lip and twirled his mother's ring.

A *very* good thing.

With a huff, Angelle turned back to her suitcase and hastily lifted a large pile of clothes from inside. She spun to carry them to the dresser and ended up ramming her foot into the wooden bedpost. *"Dang it all!"* she cursed. Or what passed for a curse from Angelle.

Face scrunched, knee bent, still avoiding his eyes, she hobbled forward with her chin held high. Having witnessed similar incidents in their ninjitsu class more times than he could count, Cane knew better than to offer any help. Nothing made her madder or more edgy than calling additional attention to her awkward mishaps. So he stood there, fighting a grin, and speculating over what made her so flustered this time.

"You do realize —" She stopped to look at her full hands, then at the closed dresser, and pursed her lips in a frown. Cane stepped forward and slid open the drawer, and she nodded. "Thank you. You do realize," she continued, slipping the clothes inside, "that small welcome on the porch was only the beginning, don't you?"

Her voice held a warning that Cane didn't understand.

The week had just started, and he knew they had plenty of acting left to do—hopefully involving more of that tight little body pressed against his. But from where he'd stood outside, things could have gone a whole lot worse. So he asked, "Huh?"

"That was just the first wave of people," Angelle explained, bumping the drawer closed with her jean-clad hip. This girl had him so twisted that even that small wiggle got his blood pumping. Cane gritted his teeth. Countless women had waltzed through his life wearing a lot less and trying a lot harder, but all this sweet thing had to do was grin, and he was turned inside out.

"What we have here is a good old-fashioned *boucherie*," she declared.

Blinking away visions of taking her on the four-post bed, Cane asked, "A boushe-what?"

"A *boucherie*," Angelle said again, this time with a smile. "It's a pig slaughter, a Cajun country thing. It's a big to-do, so we normally only hold one for special celebrations, but I guess our homecoming fits the bill. Mama said people have been here since six a.m., butchering, making *boudin* and *grattons* and hog head cheese, simmering stews, and smoking chops. And when I say people, Cane, I mean second cousins, third cousins, family friends, and more of my daddy's constituents. Not to mention Brady and his family. Most of *those* people are still in the backyard."

The fact that such an event existed, much less they reserved it for celebrations, was shocking. But not as much as discovering he *hadn't* just met the entire population of Bon Terre on her front porch.

Shaking his head, Cane couldn't help but laugh. "I own a Cajun restaurant. At crawfish boils, my family plays Cajun music. My dad used to speak Cajun-French from time to time, and I can make a mean gumbo with the best of them. I didn't think it *got* more Cajun than me. But it looks like this *city boy* is about to be schooled."

"Honey, there's *creole* Cajun and then there's *country* Cajun. Welcome to the latter."

Angelle's throaty laugh smacked him full force in the chest. It had been his intention to get her to smile—if they were about to go out there and do this thing, they needed to do it right. Which meant getting his *fiancée* to drop the uneasy, skittish vibe she suddenly had around him again. But damn if her voice and lit-up smile didn't mess with his head. Pushing those thoughts away and shoving his shoulder off the doorframe, he held out his hand. "Teach on, tour guide." And with her tiny hand in his, she led him outside.

The back of the Prejean property stretched out in one big field. Large moss-covered oaks sheltered rows of folding tables, a dozen different cook stations, and, sure enough, a throng of people. People of all ages, from babies to the elderly, sat in folding chairs talking and laughing and even more were standing, tending the food. They all seemed to stop, however, when he and Angelle strolled out the door. Smiles froze. Chatter paused. And gazes locked on their entwined hands. If he hadn't guessed before, he knew now: these people were not team Cane. If he had to wager, the whole lot, family included, were team Brady devotees.

And Cane was nothing more than the big, bad wolf messing with their *Little Red.*

Scanning the watchful crowd, Cane held in a chuckle at his bad joke. Sure enough, in the entire mass of people, he was one of three not wearing boots. And the other two were barefoot. Angelle had been right, but he doubted boots would help him now. He'd just have to win the people over. Or not. But either way, Cane hadn't survived *his* family's fractured past by letting a few whispers and looks scare him off.

A weathered gray barn stood at the back of the property. From inside, he heard the tuning of instruments. Delicious smells like he couldn't believe whacked him in the face, and since he owned a restaurant, that was saying something. As he inhaled deeply, Angelle sent him a happy grin.

"Good stuff, huh?"

Cane nodded, stepping close to a large pot of bubbling brew. "I wish Colby could see this."

When she'd first come home, it was no secret his sister had abandoned her love of Cajun cuisine; for her, there'd been too many sad memories attached to it. But thanks to Jason, Colby's first culinary love had returned with a vengeance, and now she was constantly creating unique twists on traditional recipes. If she were here today, she'd be in hog heaven. Pun intended.

Angelle stopped beside a folding table boasting boxes of fresh, crispy cracklins and selected a thick piece. Cane watched, mesmerized, as she puckered those gorgeous lips and blew on the sliver. With a flirtatious glint in her eyes, she held it up to his mouth, and he opened.

Holy crap.

He'd had cracklins before. Fried pork fat was a standard gas station treat, usually shrink-wrapped and stale as shit. But this, fresh from the pot and piping hot, was unbelievable. Cane widened his eyes, and it was possible he even moaned. It was *that* good. And as he swallowed, Angelle rewarded him with a rich, throaty laugh.

"*Ca c'est bon?*" she asked, grinning when he grabbed another handful.

He touched her nose and popped a piece in his mouth. "Good would be an understatement."

Grinning, she took a fried morsel for herself and sent the balding, overweight gentleman tending the table a wink. "Now that's what we like to hear." Then she closed her eyes as she savored the treat.

The sounds of Angelle moaning, and watching her face

soften in the throes of a foodgasm, had to be the sexiest damn thing Cane had ever seen. His pants tightened, embarrassingly so considering he knew the audience was still watching, but what pushed him over the edge was when her eyes opened. The pleasure in them was his undoing.

Feeling the weight of the crowd's disapproving stares and not giving a damn, figuring now was as good a time as any to give the people the show they clearly wanted, he grasped her hip and tugged her forward, pausing only to inhale her gasp of surprise before brushing her mouth with his.

It was like setting off a damn forest fire.

Angelle, his shocking little hellcat, pounced. Forgetting all about their audience, or maybe not giving a damn either, she wound her arms around his neck, lifted onto her toes, and kissed him back with everything she had. Cane had intended to steal a quick taste, take the edge off his craving for her, and prove their point with the town's people. But hell if he was gonna be the one to back down now. Tightening his grasp on her slim hips, he brushed his thumbs across the smooth, exposed skin near her waistband. He deepened the kiss, thrilling over her telltale shiver. Whimpering, she yanked on the hair at his nape and sucked his bottom lip into her mouth. *Hot damn.*

Okay, *now* he had to start backing down. With all her male relatives watching, not to mention the knives and axes still lying around from the butchering earlier, if Cane valued his life, he needed to wrangle control of the situation. He'd heard patience was a virtue. That was a line of bull—he'd always sucked at waiting for anything he wanted. But for Angelle, he was willing to try.

Loosening his grip on her belt loops, Cane slowed the intensity of the kiss. He smoothed the hem of her shirt down, grazed her lips one last time, and, placing his forehead against hers, inhaled through his nose. Sunflowers mixed with cayenne may be his new favorite scent. Angelle released a heavy breath, a flush blooming on her cheeks. She darted a glance at the crowd, then looking into his eyes, grinned lazily. "My goodness. If anyone doubted we were a couple before, I guess that showed them."

Cane grinned as another wave of pride rushed over him. Angelle had been with her ex for almost eight years. But the way she melted in *his* arms, responded to *his* kisses, and looked at *him* afterward, made Cane believe that everything he showed her was a new experience.

Maybe Brady never did her right. Maybe he failed to satisfy her needs. If that was the case, Cane was more than happy to correct the man's past sins. He'd gladly show his angel what real ecstasy could be like.

Hell, it'd be an honor.

Music from inside the barn began, a fast-paced tune with fiddles and accordions. Cane lifted his head, the sudden desire to dance thrumming in his veins, despite the disapproving stares from the crowd around them. Cajun dancing wasn't something he excelled at; when he was a kid, his parents had been involved in the Cajun French Music Association, but they could never get him to take the lessons. He hadn't appreciated the culture, preferring to listen to classic rock on his old Walkman whenever they took him to an event. Now an adult, Cane *did* appreciate his ancestry…but he still didn't know jack about the steps.

How hard could it be, though? He'd learned to fake just about anything with the best of them. Plus, dancing had the added bonus of holding his favorite redhead in his arms some more.

"Would you—"

But before Cane could finish the question, Angelle's gaze shifted. She tensed in his arms and took a step back as a male voice said, "It's good to see you, Angie."

Without turning, Cane knew who stood behind him. So when Angelle's shaky voice said, "You, too, Brady," it only confirmed his suspicions. But he'd be damned if he'd let her put distance between them now, especially after that kiss. And *especially* in front of her ex.

Tucking her back against his side, back where she belonged—for the rest of the week, that is—Cane turned to face the man Angelle had once considered *the one*. Sizing up her ex, he didn't get it. Brady had on a tattered baseball cap, old jeans, and cowboy boots. Certainly not the image he'd gotten of the selfish so-called "good doctor."

Their audience that had quieted earlier was now deathly silent. Brady gave Angelle a small smile that failed to hide the pain behind it, and anyone with a pair of eyes could see he still wanted her. Still loved her. Cane had expected as much. Angelle was amazing, and this town had built them up as a couple. But hell if the other man's interest didn't bring out Cane's inner caveman. And damn if that didn't grate on his nerves even more.

So the two had a past. She chose to walk away from it. Even if she changed her mind, it shouldn't matter. This thing between them was a hoax. It wasn't real. But that didn't keep him from pressing a lingering kiss on the top of her head anyway. And telling himself it was for the sake of the charade.

Her ex nodded at the gesture and took a long pull off his beer. Swallowing, he held out his hand and lifted his mouth in a close approximation of a smile. "Brady Doucet. Real pleased to meet you."

"Cane Robicheaux," he said, staring at the outstretched hand for a half-beat before shaking it. "Likewise."

Chapter Seven

This was really happening.

Brady and Cane were actually standing toe-to-toe, shaking hands, and her entire hometown (or what felt like it) was keeping watch. Angelle knew this moment would come. Heck, she'd even tried to prepare herself for it. But no amount of forethought could've lessened the shock of seeing her ex approach while she was still reeling from Cane's toe-tingling kiss. On instinct, she'd shuffled back a step, guilt worms snaking through her insides at the flash of hurt in Brady's eyes.

At Cane's instinctive response, they locked in shock with the rest of her.

Of course to everyone watching, he was her fiancé. It made sense for him to stake his claim. But what Angie couldn't figure out was if Cane was just playing the part for the busybody crowd or if it were more. Was he that good of an actor…or could the playboy of Magnolia Springs actually be jealous over *her?*

Where exactly did the game end?

And did it even matter?

Cane's kisses were phenomenal. Better than chocolate, horses, and Channing Tatum rolled into one. But it proved that he had *beaucoup* experience. If she didn't keep the wall between truth and fiction firmly in place, her poor virginal heart would be left decimated in the end.

Brady cleared his throat and Angelle realized they'd been standing in awkward silence for way too long. Subtly, she tried releasing the breath she'd been holding—it came out as a harsh bark of laughter. When both men turned to eyeball her, she lifted her mouth in a nervous smile so wide it almost hurt. "*So*, Brady, how's the residency going?"

Why she was attempting small talk was anyone's guess. It'd be best, for everyone involved, if either he or they made a quick getaway. Baby steps into the world of discomfort that awaited them this week would be a good thing. But apparently, you can take the girl out of the country, but you can't take the ingrained country manners out of the girl. Mama hadn't raised her to be impolite. Not even out of self-preservation.

Brady rocked back on the heels of his cowboy boots. "It's good. The new hospital in Lafayette is state-of-the-art; you should come by and check it out." He glanced at Cane. "You know, if the two of you have time."

"Yeah, we'll do that." Angelle felt Cane watching her, but she didn't look up. She couldn't. "It must be nice working so close to home. I'm sure your mama's happy about that."

Really, Angelle? That's what you come up with? You suck at small talk.

"Sure." With a tight-lipped smile, Brady lifted his beer bottle as if to take another sip, then stopped to stare at the red and white label. "Things sure aren't how I'd planned, but it's nice being back all the same."

Pressing the bottle to his lips, he took a long pull as Angelle winced. This was the most awkward conversation in the history of the universe. Nine months ago, she hadn't thought it could get worse than telling this man she didn't want to marry him. Particularly since she did so with an entire auditorium of friends and family there as witnesses. But wearing another man's ring and faking a comfortable conversation while many of those same people looked on broke Angelle's heart. She could only imagine what it was doing to Brady.

This was why she'd been so terrified to come home. It was never about her ex causing a scene or making trouble; Brady was too much of a gentleman to do that. No, what worried her was *this*—seeing him again, noting the pain in his eyes and the hope in her family's, and having the pressure to make everyone else happy cause *her* will to dissolve. There was no doubt Brady was the safe route. The expected and easy course. It was what the town wanted for her, what her parents wanted.

It just wasn't what *she* wanted.

Cane squeezed her side, perhaps sensing her torment, and she leaned into his strength. She needed it.

"So how did you two kids meet?" Brady winced as he asked, clearly as uncomfortable with prolonging this torture as she was, yet trying just as hard to be polite. If one of them didn't call an end to this madness soon, she could very well go insane.

Wanting to get it over with as soon as possible, Angelle opened her mouth and answered, "At his restaurant," at the same time Cane replied, "At a club."

Brady's eyes grew as wide as hay bales—or, more accurately, as wide as the two gaping holes in their story.

First, it was obvious they'd forgotten to discuss a few vital details for their ruse. Namely, details about *them* as a couple. Where they met, how and when he proposed, when they planned to get married. None of those things had even entered her mind before…but they were flashing in neon now.

Second, anyone who knew Angelle would know the club scene wasn't for her. Too loud, too crowded, too full of opportunities to bust her ass in a klutzy fit on the dance floor. One would assume her fiancé would know that. Oops.

Cane's amused brown eyes met hers, and Angelle wanted to slap him. This wasn't *funny*. She forced a smile even as she felt her cheeks warm—no doubt they were glowing hot pink about now; lying was so not her forte—and turned to Brady. "Actually—"

"Actually it's both." Cane tugged her close and pressed his lips against her hair. Grateful for the save, and curious to hear how on earth he would answer, Angelle stared up in wonder. He winked. "One night this sexy redhead walked into the restaurant I own to meet my sisters. I couldn't take my eyes off her, but who could blame me? She's gorgeous."

Angelle felt her cheeks grow hotter, but this time it had nothing to do with telling a lie. Cane chuckled. "Anyway, I overheard them talk her into heading to a club up the road, so I followed her like the infatuated stalker I am and asked for a dance. The rest, as they say, is history."

The man was *good*. Too good, to be honest. The story he painted. The deep, rich voice he used telling it. Angie blinked and turned back to her ex, forcibly breaking the spell Cane had woven.

"That's…nice." Brady shoved his hand deep in his pocket, his familiar eyes dull beneath the rim of his ball cap. "Well, I guess I'll let you two get on back to your conversation. I just wanted to come by and say hello. It's been a while, Angie, but you look real good." His mouth lifted in a pained smile as he took a step back. "Happy."

"Oh, Brady, I don't—"

He shook his head, cutting her off. "No, I'm glad. You being happy is what I wanted." He looked to Cane and said, "You be sure to take care of her."

The words were well intentioned; Angie knew that. But they still rankled. She didn't *need* anyone to take care of her. That's what the people in this town never understood. Somewhere along the way she'd lost her voice, but now she was more than the girl they once knew. Not too much more, but a definite work in progress. She was gearing up to say exactly that when Cane squeezed her hand and replied, "I like to think we take care of each *other*."

Surprised—it was as if he'd stolen the words right from her head—Angelle looked up, and a mischievous grin crossed his face. "As I'm sure you know, this woman's a spitfire. If she had to, I figure she can handle just about anything on her own. But as for treating her right…that I fully intend to do."

His voice came out steady and clear like a promise. A veiled promise, because Angelle had the impression she was missing something. Like his words held a double meaning. What it was, she hadn't a clue.

Brady nodded slowly, then with a released breath, held out his hand. "Nice meeting you, Cane."

Her fake fiancé shook it and said, "Same goes."

The two men exchanged a meaningful look, one she couldn't begin to decipher, and then with a final whisper of a smile at Angelle, Brady turned and walked away.

"You okay, darlin'?" Cane placed a knuckle under her chin so he could study her eyes. "That sucked ass, but it's over, right? The first big showdown is in the bag."

He jostled her shoulder in an attempt to lift her sagging spirits, and she sighed. "Yeah, you're right. It is, and actually, that went better than it could have, thanks to your quick thinking. Maybe now Brady can move on." She hoped with all her heart that he would. Her ex really was a fine man, and he'd make some lucky woman an amazing husband. That woman just wasn't her.

"Exactly," Cane said. "So enough with the gloom and

doom. Let's get to work restoring that gorgeous smile of yours. I hear it's a celebration. The black sheep of Bon Terre has returned, along with her city-boy fiancé. That kind of gossip doesn't come to town every day. Such an occasion requires good eats, and my nose informs me we've got plenty of that to choose from."

Nose in the air, he sniffed audibly, and despite the pain and discomfort of the last few minutes, Angelle couldn't help but laugh. Cane winked. "See, there's that smile I was looking for. Lights up every damn room you walk into, sweetheart. Now what do you say we get this outsider some grub?"

· · ·

Twinkling lights strung among the trees clicked on as the sunlight faded. Light from inside the warm house glowed against the darkening sky. But even though there was a chill in the air, Angelle wasn't budging. She enjoyed watching Cane in this setting. About an hour before, Ryan had pulled him into a hand of *bourre,* a Cajun card game that's a blend of poker and spades. Troy was there, too, only slightly less welcoming—and a lot more intense. He was never rude to the man she'd brought home, merely watchful and aloof. Distant. But if it bothered Cane, she sure couldn't tell. He'd been telling jokes for hours, teasing with the best of them. Once, he'd even got Troy to crack a smile.

From her perch on the old double swing, his claim of the *gris-gris* being cast on his hand reached her ears. *A fish out of water, my foot*, she thought with an amused grin. From the pieces she'd puzzled together from her own sly observations and Colby and Sherry's nuggets of intel, Angie knew Cane was used to being in charge. He liked order, for things to stay the same. Being out of his element like this had to be a new experience. But when the half-empty bottle of Patron made its way to Cane, he took a giant swig without hesitation.

The country revealed a new side of Cane Robicheaux, unexpected nuances to his personality and character. The more she observed, the more she realized he resembled the yin-yang tattoo he'd inked on his skin. Cane was a duality of light and dark, tough and sweet, bad boy and protector. His country side openly smiled, seemed more relaxed, and watched her with hungry eyes. Okay, so the hungry eyes were far from new, but the determined fire beneath them was. And they brought a shiver to her skin that had zilch to do with the cool air.

As for Cane's hidden protector, well, that was perhaps the most shocking of all. The last five months had revealed how he was with his sisters, but seeing him defend *her*, protect *her*, had Angelle's heart beating a strange rhythm in her chest. She'd been protected all her life, but it always made her feel less than. Like no one believed she was able to do things herself or saw her as a growing woman. But with Cane, it was the exact opposite. With him, she was 100 percent woman, and when he stood up for her, it felt like *support*. Like caring.

Earlier, when a snooty cousin had approached, making a quip about Angelle being the Bon Terre equivalent of a runaway bride, Cane hadn't hesitated to defend her. "She's making a good life for herself," he'd said, wrapping both arms around her waist. He'd smiled proudly and tugged her against his solid chest. "And I'm sure as hell glad she ran. I wouldn't have met my angel otherwise."

He seemed to like calling her that, his *angel*. With the way she'd hurt Brady and left her mama to deal with the fallout, Angelle was pretty sure she was far from angelic—but hearing him call her that made her feel special all the same. Cherished.

And that worried her more than Troy's reaction.

Angelle couldn't allow herself to forget this was only a

farce, a charade for her family. This wasn't the beginning of something real. It was possible there was more to the man than she'd originally thought, but how much of it was truth and how much was fiction—or painted by the memory of his yummy kisses? She was on a slippery slope, in danger of falling for her own lie.

A loud *smack* startled her as the back screen door hit the siding. A three-foot-tall bundle of energy zipped past, Angelle's mama tailing right behind screaming, "Sadie, *t'es nu!*"

Angie laughed out loud. Truthfully, her godchild *wasn't* naked. Sadie had on a hot pink bathrobe with big purple polka dots. But if the feisty four-year-old had been naked, it wouldn't have been the first time Troy's daughter streaked through a family gathering. Covering her mouth so as not to encourage her niece's antics, Angelle watched her mother chase her around the yard. Apparently little Sadie wasn't ready for bed.

"You've had your fun, now it's time to get inside," Mama cajoled, catching her breath as she leaned against a folding chair. "It's cold cold out here, *cher*. You need to put some darn clothes on."

Cane's eyebrows snapped together at her mother's choice of words. In the country, they often doubled words for emphasis. Like right now, it wasn't *very* cold outside—it was cold cold. The delicious jambalaya they'd eaten earlier wasn't *really* good—it was good good. Angie had learned that was a unique turn of the tongue after returning from her first fire and saying it'd been "hot hot."

The boys at the firehouse had gotten a kick out of that.

Sadie shot past Eva's attempted grasp and headed straight for the *bourre* table. Angelle's sister-in-law slumped beside her on the swing and declared with a sigh, "That girl could try the patience of a nun." She shook her head at Sadie skirting her daddy's clutches. "But I love her to pieces. Do you know what she told me yesterday, when we were preparing for all this?" Angelle shook her head. "She said she couldn't stop nagging everyone because her imaginary friends wouldn't play with her."

Angie snorted. "That's Troy's daughter, all right."

"And don't I know it." Eva grumbled, but the love she had for her family was plain as day on her face. "I told her, *cher*, you do know they're pretend, don't you? You can tell them what to do. But that girl stuck to her story. Stubborn as a mule, just like her daddy." She shook her head and glanced back at her giggling child. "You've gotta respect her creativity, though."

Angelle placed her hands on her thighs, prepared to jump into the fray. "Wait until she becomes a teenager," she teased. "That was when Troy really reached his stride."

Eva groaned as Angie pushed to her feet, but that was when young Sadie rendered her assistance moot by jumping onto Cane's jean-clad lap. For his part, her big bad fiancé appeared floored for a nanosecond, then scooped the little girl closer, fixed her robe modestly over her tiny legs, and proceeded to show her his cards.

None of which would have been surprising, had the two met before. Or Sadie made climbing onto strangers a normal occurrence. But they hadn't. Sadie had been running with her cousins all afternoon while Cane received the grand tour. And her niece, while being a wild child, was a *shy* wild child. At least when it came to strangers.

Angelle knew Cane was good with children. She'd seen his interactions with Emma. But seeing the inked-up tough guy hold the little girl who owned *her* heart, and having that same little girl look up at him with her biggest, toothiest smile, made something in Angie's chest clench and then loosen.

The feeling of crumbling defenses.

Mama walked up, releasing an exhausted sigh. "Tag, you're it," she said, wedging her hips between her daughter and daughter-in-law. "That girl's done tuckered me out."

Eva wrapped an arm around her mother-in-law and squeezed. "Thank you, Mama." Sliding Angelle a grin, she added, "But it appears Sadie's in good hands for now."

"Hmm." Mama pressed her lips together as she regarded the card table. "That's a mighty intriguing fiancé you have there, *petite fille*. Don't be thinking your daddy and I didn't notice the tattoos."

Wincing, Angie bit her lip and waited for the inquisition. She sure as heck had battled everyone else that afternoon.

From Ryan's, *Why a firefighter?* To his wife's, *Do you know how dangerous that is?*

Her Papa's quiet, *Why Magnolia Springs?* And her grams's, *When are you coming home?*

And the big, unasked question that prompted them all: *Is this all Cane's doing?*

But it was just the first day. The hard part was over; everyone saw that she'd moved on from Brady. They had the rest of the week to realize her other changes were more than a quarter-life crisis or the influence of a bad boy. That this was *her*. Angelle Prejean 2.0.

But if she could do anything to alleviate her parents' fears now, she would.

"Mama, he's more than you think," she said, reaching across Eva to touch her mother's shoulder. "He's not Dylan." *And I'm not Amber.*

Her mother nodded slowly, seeming to study the man in question closely. Angie's gaze drifted back to the table. Cane's dark head was lowered so Sadie could whisper in his ear. He threw his head back in a laugh as the little girl giggled. Mama's voice was soft as she asked, "But is he good people, *cher*? Does he treat you right?"

Watching her niece, Angelle thought about the times Cane had teased *her*, too. Joking and flirting, making her smile. How he'd stepped up to help her this week with minimal questions asked, and defended her when her own family's questions were too harsh. So, even as she fought to rebuild her crumbled defenses, Angelle nodded. "Yeah, Mama. He does."

Eva nodded and stood abruptly, causing the swing to rock beneath them. "Then that's all I need to hear. Personally, any man who looks like that *and* can wrangle my child is a keeper."

Eva sent Angie a wink and thanked Mama for bathing Sadie, then walked over to retrieve her spirited daughter. Cane nodded at something Eva told him and accepted a hug from Sadie before sending the girl on her merry little way. Troy shot him a civil nod, then promptly returned to his hand of cards. But her fake fiancé sought out Angie, and when their gazes met across the yard, the dimple in his cheek flashed in a grin.

Angelle's heart rate escalated. *I'm in a heap of trouble.*

Chapter Eight

"It's tradition," Angelle explained the next night as she trekked the familiar path to her brother's house holding a tutu-wearing teddy bear. "The night before Thanksgiving, everyone goes out. I've never stopped to wonder why, especially since so many of us wake up early to cook." She shrugged her shoulders and then quickened her steps as the cool evening air snaked across her skin. "It's just what we've always done."

Cane easily lengthened his long-legged stride to keep up. "And you're sure you don't want to go out, too? You've been gone a long time. If you want to hang out with your friends, it's okay."

She shook her head, stifling a smile at the crunch of motorcycle boots on gravel. It appeared one day of taunts over sneakers was her fiancé's limit. "I saw the important people yesterday, and I'll see them again tomorrow. Eva and Troy deserve a night out." Twisting around at a rhythmic *beep-beep-beep*, she jogged to the side of the road to let Lacey pass. The crazy girl cranked the radio up and sang along—loud, proud, and off-key—and Angelle grinned as she waved to her cousin's retreating taillights. "Besides, spending time with my godchild is one of the things I miss most about being home. I need some Nanny time with my girl."

Cane's hand brushed against hers and he took it. Warmth seeped into her skin. "That I can understand. I remember when Emma was Sadie's age, full of stories, wanting to give me manicures, endless energy." He glanced over and smiled. "Pretty much the same as she is today."

"God, don't tell Troy that," she said, the scent of leather filling her head. "My brother thinks Sadie will calm down once she enters kindergarten. We're guessing he forgot what a hellion he used to be. Daddy's always said payback is the Lord's to give, and it looks like Troy's getting his comeuppance."

A deep laugh rumbled in Cane's chest. The sound was low and dark, and did funny things to her tummy. Things she rather enjoyed. The Magnolia Springs playboy was back, black jacket and motorcycle boots in place, but after last night, he no longer terrified her. In fact, the whole getup was now a surprising turn on, and mixed with the woodsy notes of his cologne, Angelle was almost dizzy. Instead of running, she wanted to press her nose against the smooth tan skin of his neck and get a good whiff. And then maybe lick it.

Inexplicably giddy. That was the best description for how Angelle felt as she tromped up her brother's stairs. Her chest held a lightness, a bounce was in her step, and she couldn't stop smiling—despite the worrisome niggles pricking her brain. It'd been the same way all afternoon.

The boucherie hadn't ended until after two a.m., so she and Cane had slept in and then lazed around the house, snacking on leftovers and playing *bourre*. She'd thoroughly trounced him every time, but Cane had taken it in stride, shaking his head and shooting her that flirty grin. Tempting her with each dimple flash to drag his fine self to her bedroom and engage in another round of toe-tingling kisses. The only thing that held her back—*other* than her ultra-conservative parents in the next room—was the neon-lit question blinking behind her eyelids. *Exactly how far is too far?*

Angelle wasn't ready to make love. At least, she didn't *think* she was. She still believed what she'd told Sherry, that the holy trinity had to be present before she gave up her V-card: passion, excitement, and for it to *feel* right. The first two she and Cane pushed to the extreme. The third was harder to define.

On the drive up, Angie had resolved to experience a taste of that passion. It would be silly, considering the circumstances, not to reap a small benefit from this crazy situation. But did a taste stop at kisses? Or could her innocent heart withstand letting a man as experienced as Cane go where no man had gone before?

A cool hand sliding along the base of her spine shook Angelle from her thoughts. "You okay?" Cane stepped close, filling her head with his delicious scent again. "You seem like you're a thousand miles away."

Or just back in bed, ogling your beautiful inked body.

"I'm fine." She smiled brightly as she knocked on her brother's door. Immediately, rapid, thumping footsteps approached and she asked, "You sure you're ready for this?"

Cane set his mouth to her ear. "Darlin', I've got this in the bag."

A shiver ran down her spine. The deep notes of his voice implied he meant more than just a night of babysitting, a night more in line with her previous thoughts. But while she was busy wrestling with the courage to ask *what*, the door opened and a strawberry-blond head stuck out.

"Sugar girl!" Setting aside her confusing, non-existent sex life, Angelle held out her arms…and watched as her niece shot right past them.

"You're here!" Sadie exclaimed, slamming into Cane's tree trunk of a thigh and wrapping her skinny arms around it.

Angelle frowned, and Cane shrugged his massive shoulders as he bent to pick up the girl. So he had an effect on women. Of *all* ages. She knew—probably better than anyone—how charismatic the man could be, and she'd be lying if she said this sweet side to the town bad boy wasn't a turn on. It was.

But she was *Nanny*. She came bearing gifts!

"What, no love for me?" she asked, shaking the tutu-wearing teddy bear in her hands. Sadie took it with a happy, toothy grin and settled back against Cane's broad chest.

I knew I should've brought chocolate.

"Here, let me see that teddy bear," Cane said, taking the stuffed animal from her niece's tiny hands. He sent Angelle a dimpled grin as he examined it, then pursed his lips. "You know, Sadie, this is a mighty fine bear. Tutu and all. I'm thinking maybe I'll keep it. You didn't *really* want this, did you?"

"Yes I do!" she protested, stealing the toy back from his hands. "That's *my* bear, Mr. Cane. Nanny brought it for *me*." She twisted around with a four-year-old pout. "Right, Nanny?"

Angelle smiled, her heart completely melted and dripping on her shoes. "Yep, I'm sorry, Mr. Cane, but that bear is for my sugar girl."

He huffed an exasperated sigh and then leaned close to whisper in her niece's ear. Sadie nodded, holding out her hands, and Angelle gladly accepted her soft weight. Hugging her close, she met Cane's eyes over Sadie's head and mouthed, *Thank you.*

Cane winked. "Shall we, ladies?" He held his hand out to the opened door, and they walked inside.

Troy and Eva's home always smelled like Lemon Pledge.

It was one more thing that never changed, and Angelle hoped never would. She set Sadie down and the little girl scampered off on bare feet, hugging her bear. It was nice to be around family again.

After hanging up her coat, Angie strolled down the hall vowing never to let the ghost of a failed relationship keep her away again for so long. She searched the living room and kitchen for her brother and sister-in-law, and then realized Cane was still back at the entryway, looking at pictures.

"Uh, please don't tell me they hung up that one from Christmas," she said, shoving her hands in her back pockets as she retracted her steps. "I plead the fifth on that outfit."

Cane transferred his gaze to her. "Brady was a groomsman at your brother's wedding?"

Surprised by the confused look in his eyes, Angelle's smile dropped and she glanced at the photo of her brother's bridal party. "Our fathers are friends. By the time Troy and Eva married, we'd been together for four years. Brady was, and still is, considered part of the family."

With that same strange look, Cane leaned his back against the wall of frames. "That complicates things now that you're broken up."

"Well, yeah, but what can I do? It is what it is," she said with a shrug. "It'd be easier if Brady faded into my past, like a normal ex, but that's not the cards I've been dealt. I can either choose to whine and cry about it, or I can make the best of the situation." When he seemed to marvel at that, studying her with an intensity that made her nervous, she shrugged again and added, "Or I can go with door number three and invent a fake fiancé."

Cane craned an eyebrow and chuckled low in his throat. "There is always that."

Looping her arm around his much beefier one, Angelle left the memories behind her and walked down the hall. For the rest of the night, she didn't want to think about Brady or disappointing anyone.

She just wanted to be a normal girl, babysitting her naked-loving, wild-child niece with her handsome fake fiancé. That wasn't too much to ask, was it?

Eva bustled through after they'd taken a seat on the plush sofa. "Y'all, I'm so sorry I'm running late. It's been so long since we've gone out I couldn't find a single thing to wear. Does this look okay?"

She spun around, showing off a pair of dark wash jeans, red boots, and matching V-neck sweater, and Angelle replied, "Fabulous as always," completely meaning it. She'd kill to have her sister-in-law's voluptuous figure. Sadie shuffled back into the room and sprang up onto the sofa, wiggling her bottom between her aunt and Cane.

"I've been telling her the same thing for the last hour," her brother said, coming down the hall. Troy kissed his wife's head and then swatted her backside as he passed behind her. "You should see our bedroom. Her entire side of the closet is now sprawled across the floor."

Eva rolled her eyes. "Honey, this mama needs a night out, and she wants to look good doing it." She slipped her license out of her wallet and shoved it in her back pocket. "Angie, you're a lifesaver. You too, Cane. Consider it a given that we'll return the favor as soon as you two start popping out babies."

Heat filled Angie's cheeks at Eva's suggestive eyebrow wiggle. Images flooded her mind. Not so much the popping out part, but the actions that would precede it. She squirmed in her seat and Cane smirked beside her.

Troy cleared his throat, apparently equally uncomfortable with allusions to his little sister's sex life. Or at least her sex life with Cane, a man he didn't know, didn't like, and wasn't Brady. The usual humor faded from his light blue eyes as he coolly assessed the man beside her. "Anyway we shouldn't be out too late," he said a tad gruffly, removing a stack of bills from his wallet. He set them on the counter. "Here's money for pizza, and there's Coke, beer, and wine in the fridge."

Cane pushed to his feet. "Actually, if you don't mind, I was thinking I'd run to the store up the road and cook dinner." He glanced down and said, "That is, if I can find me a chef's helper."

Sadie climbed to a standing position on the sofa and thrust her hand in the air. "Me! Me, Mr. Cane! Mama says I'm a great cheff-er, don't ya, Mama?"

Eva nodded with a smile. "She's the best."

"Is that right?" Cane sunk to his knees so they were eye-level. "Must be my lucky day. Do you know I happen to own a restaurant? Maybe one day you can come and work for me. What do you think about that?"

Sadie shook her head solemnly. "Thanks, but I'm gonna be a fairy princess and live in Disney World."

Cane grinned. "That does sound like more fun."

Smiling at the two of them, Angelle shifted her gaze to her brother. Troy was stubborn; there would be no winning him over with one adorable conversation with his kid. But Cane had taken a first step. The ease of tension in Troy's face and the conspiratorial wink Eva shot her was proof of that. Angie bit back a smile of victory.

One small step for Cane. One giant step for Project Pickle.

• • •

Women were his weakness. Cane could admit it. And when they were adorable and pint-sized, he was a goner. In some ways, he bonded better with kids because they were safe. He could be himself and not worry about the fallout. The problem was that after only twenty-four hours, Sadie already had him wrapped around her little finger—and she knew it.

Had he learned nothing from dealing with Emma?

Grinning, Cane strolled back into the kitchen, putting the dirty dishes in the sink. Dinner had been a raving success. It had kept the kid entertained, kept him from going stir-crazy, and it showed Angelle once again that he wasn't a complete ass. Since she'd entered his truck yesterday, the game had changed. His goal had shifted. No longer was this only about getting her out of his system, though that did have to happen, the sooner the better. But now, he didn't just want her comfortable enough to explore their explosive attraction. Cane realized he wanted to let Angelle *in*.

The woman who fascinated him from afar was even better up close: feisty and sweet, vulnerable and strong, and when she let her guard down, captivating. He wasn't ready to give her up completely at the end of the week, but since a real relationship was off the table, that left friendship. A female friend would be a new experience for Cane, but Angelle already broke every other rule of his. What was one more?

Ensuring she didn't get close enough to get hurt was going to be the issue. It would take a balancing act, but she volunteered with his best friend. She lived with his baby sister and was close with the other. Friendship, as long as he maintained a few key walls, should be harmless. *As long as love stays the hell out of it.*

"Whew! That girl is a mess and a half," Angelle said, walking into the room, "but God, I love her." Smiling, she scooted onto the barstool and propped her chin on her hand. "Good call, by the way, on the compromise. If that's really all it takes to get her to sleep—one messed-up bedtime story and an off-key song—then I'm *beaucoup* impressed. You're like the kid whisperer."

Her smile widened and Cane laughed, but what she'd actually said was anyone's guess. He'd been too distracted by the creamy expanse of skin exposed on her neck to listen. At some point between Sadie's room and the kitchen, Angelle must've stopped in the bathroom because her long red hair lay piled on her head, rebellious strands curling around her face. Innocent and sexy. That was Angelle. It was a conflicting blend uniquely her, and it pulled him in every time.

Clearing his throat, he turned to the refrigerator. "Want a glass of wine? I believe we earned it after that performance."

A *screech* of wood against tile preceded her laugh. "I'd say so. You're gonna have to tell me where you came up with that fairy tale. It was like a disturbing mix of Rumpelstiltskin, *Cinderella*, The Powerpuff Girls, and *Star Wars*." She slid up beside him and bumped his hip so she could lean inside the fridge. "And actually, bartender, you should know I'm more of a beer girl."

Cane smirked as he took a longneck for himself. "Two little sisters, a dad with a rather strange sense of humor, and Emma—*that's* where the story came from." He twisted the top off his beer, handed it to Angelle, and took the one from her hands. Unscrewing it, he lifted his arm to pitch the two bottle caps in the trash when she latched onto his arm.

"Don't."

Eyebrow lifted, Cane opened his hand and glanced at the discards. "Did you want to keep these for something?"

Angelle chewed the corner of her lip. "Yeah. I like keeping the tops. My…" She trailed off and shook her head, lips pressed firmly together. "I used to make crafts with them. I don't anymore," she clarified, "and even when I did, I was never very good at it. But it's just something I do." She shrugged her shoulders and looked at the caps. "A good memory."

Sensing there was a story there, more than likely one tied to the mysterious sister he was growing more and more curious about, Cane dropped them in her hand and then nodded toward the living room. "Let's go take a load off."

On the short walk to the sofa, he thought about the picture he'd seen in Ryan's room. He'd stared at it again this afternoon. The longer he looked, the more he was convinced that if he wanted to unlock the secrets surrounding the woman who ran hot and cold and in the opposite direction, despite clearly being attracted to him, the key lay buried in her past. Settling down on the floor, his back against the sofa, beer on the coffee table, Cane said, "I like your family. They might not like *me* all that much…"

Angelle winced. "Sorry about that. They'll come around. You're just—not what they were expecting." She eyed the tattoo peeking out from his sleeve. "But hey, you've already got Lacey, Sadie, and Eva in your corner. Troy will come around eventually. I predict you'll have them all eating out of the palm of your hand by the end of the week." She rolled her eyes and shot him a grin. "Then they can be mad at me for *two* failed engagements."

Her nose scrunched adorably and she took a sip of her beer. Cane waited until she'd set her bottle down and began absentmindedly playing with the caps to ask, "So tell me more about them. What was your childhood like? Clearly, you were a surprise."

"You caught that, huh?" Angelle's quick whiskey laugh curled around him. "Yeah, Mama and Daddy were into their forties when they *popped* me out. Ryan and I like to say it's the tale of two parents. He got Daddy younger, an attorney, and a lot more laid-back. By the time I came around, he had wisps of gray and was already in politics. They were still amazing, don't get me wrong, but I definitely grew up believing I had to be beyond reproach." She twisted onto her hip to face him. "Living in a small town means everyone knows your faults and mistakes. I just never allowed myself to have any. Or any that people could see, that is."

A world of information lay in that revelation. Feeling like

he was finally getting somewhere, Cane decided to encourage her by telling a little of his own story. "I know a thing or two about small town gossip," he shared.

Her head tilted. "You do?"

Cane nodded, surprised even as he did so that he was about to admit this. "By the time you came to Magnolia Springs, most of it had died down. But at one time, whispering about my family was more entertaining than an afternoon soap opera."

He watched her reaction carefully, and when she seemed genuinely confused, a knot in his chest loosened. *Sherry must still not know.* He'd sure threatened enough people within an inch of their life, and it looked as though it had worked. If his baby sister *had* heard the gossip about their father and the town librarian, she'd never have kept it to herself. She was too emotional for that. He may've failed Colby, but Cane was glad to know he'd protected at least one of the women in his life from the truth.

"The Robicheaux family is an institution," Angelle said, eyebrows furrowed. "What on earth could people possibly gossip about?"

"Plenty, but most of it was about my dad's affair."

The words came out sharp and clinical. Deadpan. He'd already processed the pain and had actually forgiven his father for the consequences. But it didn't mean the effects didn't haunt him every day.

The knot in his chest loosened a bit more at Angelle's sharp gasp of surprise. Taking a long pull off his beer, Cane propped his elbow against the soft sofa cushion and faced her. "Dad tried keeping it a secret, of course, but in a town as small as Magnolia Springs, everyone's listening. Everyone's watching. And when I was twenty, a guy who'd had one too many spilled the beans."

Her pink lips parted and her hand rested on top of his.

"God, how awful. Did your sisters know?"

Cane stared at her long, slender fingers, wishing he could answer differently. "Sherry doesn't. And if I have anything to do with it, she never will." He lifted his eyes to hers. "You can't tell her."

The soft skin between her eyebrows furrowed. "Of course not. I'm not in the habit of hurting my friends for no reason."

Cane let out a sigh and dropped his gaze again. He knew that. The last two days proved she was more kind, more loving, than any woman he'd met. "I know. It's just that after I confronted my father, I vowed to shelter my sisters from ever hearing the truth. The last thing I wanted was for them to go through the same thing I did. To have that stupid perfect family bubble we thought we'd lived in shattered. But I screwed up — Colby found out. That's what sent her packing years ago. My starry-eyed sister was so scared she'd fall for someone like Dad that she gave up on love and left home. That's *my* fault. And if Jason hadn't broken through her walls, she'd still be a mess because of it."

His hand fisted on the sofa, and Angelle's clenched around it. "It's *not* your fault."

Cane scoffed and took another sip of his drink.

Where in the hell is this coming from?

Talking about his past didn't happen. Same for his personal life. Hell, he hadn't even told Jason about everything until this year, and only because he was cornered. He'd just meant to share a piece of the past, enough to encourage Angelle to do the same. Not act like a damn volcano, spewing family shit all over the room.

The story of his life was told in ink, not words. The koi fish swimming up his ribs. Against the current. Fighting to overpower his past. The yin-yang on his chest. The dark and light. The balance between pain and peace. His father had been a good man who made a mistake, but it had ripped his family apart. That same darkness lived inside of Cane. Inside everyone. The difference was that he refused to give it opportunity to let loose.

Angelle shook his hand, gaining his attention. "It's *not*. You couldn't control your dad. Those were his mistakes, not yours. I'm sure Colby doesn't blame you."

He slid his hand away, immediately missing her soft touch, the warmth of her skin. But the lack of it was a good thing. It reminded him that he couldn't allow her to get too close. Intimacy, feeling too much, meant pain. This conversation alone should've been reminder enough.

"You're right," he told her, lifting the beer bottle to his mouth. "She doesn't blame me. *I* do."

Chapter Nine

What do you say to a man so stubbornly fixated on pointless self-guilt? Angelle wanted to slap Cane upside the head and cuddle him at the same time. It was clear she wasn't going to change his mind, at least not tonight, and it wasn't her place to involve Colby. But she needed to do *something*. She'd seen Cane half-naked and cocky at Best Abs, sweaty and arrogant in a gym, and rocked out and bigheaded on a stage with his guitar, but *vulnerable* never even entered the same mental airspace as the town bad boy...until now.

Now, vulnerable was the best description for how Cane looked as he sat across from her in Troy's living room. He appeared as shocked by his confession as she was, but she was glad he'd shared it. It gave her a better understanding of what made the man tick. Why he acted the way he did. Cane Robicheaux wasn't just a stubborn ass who had women dropping at his feet. He was a protective warrior who'd go to battle for those he loved.

That knowledge was dangerous to her psyche, her hormones, and her heart, because to heck with her five-month-old crush. If Angie hadn't already been in full-blown lust with her fake fiancé, she darn well was now.

"You know, I grew up with a protective sibling, too."

Cane set his empty bottle on the table and raised an eyebrow. "Yeah, I met your brothers, remember?"

Picking up a bottle cap, she shook her head. "No. I don't mean Ryan or Troy. They're *over*protective. I meant my sister, Amber." Angelle traced the ridges of the metal top, feeling his gaze heavy on her cheek. "She was the one who used to make the crafts with these. Flip-flops, picture frames, jewelry, candles—you name it—she made it with bottle caps. She'd sneak around collecting them at family parties and events and then sell her stuff at school and craft fairs. I was young—and terrified of the hot glue gun—but she made me her honorary helper." Angie grinned at the memory. "I thought it was the coolest job in the world, and I hocked her stuff everywhere I went. I fully believed they were the most beautiful, special items ever in existence. And they were. Because *Amber* made them."

Cane was quiet for a moment, but then he said, "Sounds like she was pretty amazing." Angelle raised her head at the softness of his voice, and the use of the word *was*. Her eyes studied his, and he nodded at her unspoken question. "You mentioned in the ride over you had a sibling that *had been* ten years older. The past tense and the fact that neither of your brothers fit the bill had me wondering. Then I found a picture in your brother's room."

A small smile turned the corners of her mouth. "I think I know the one you're talking about. Ryan's first start for UL Lafayette. That was in the middle of Amber's eccentric phase, as Mama liked to call it. That girl was a mess, a total wild child. A lot like Sherry, actually. She was forever getting into trouble, laughing, acting crazy. She was never scared to take a chance."

Angie flipped her wrist to look at her tattoo.

Chance.

"Sounds exactly like Sherry," Cane confirmed, his voice sounding closer than it had before. A tan finger brushed over the faded lines of her old scar. "So what happened to her?"

The muscles of Angelle's stomach tightened, whether it was from the contact, the memory, or both, she didn't know. She swallowed hard past a lump of emotion. "Her first year in college she made new friends. Before that, she was rebellious, but she never pushed it too far. But then she stopped coming home so much, got a tattoo and some piercings, and Mama and Daddy didn't like it. Her grades stayed up, so there wasn't much they could do, but Lord, they sure tried. And once Dylan entered the picture, it was all over."

Her mind conjured an image of the boy who'd stolen her sister's heart.

"Amber was head over heels in love with the epitome of a bad boy." She gave Cane a small smile and said, "You two could've been twins. Dark hair, tattoos, motorcycle…he was Daddy's worst nightmare for his little girl."

Cane rubbed the stubble along his jaw. "Then I guess that makes me nightmare number two. At least that helps explain the lukewarm reaction."

Angelle sighed. "That's definitely part of it." It had also been one of the reasons she'd stressed about bringing him home. But what else could she have done? Her brain had already short-circuited by that point, slipping out his name. "As for Dylan, I don't know if he was that bad of a guy. I mean, I was only nine, and pretty much caught in the middle every time my sister brought him around. But he never talked down to me or anything. Never treated me like an annoying kid sister. What mattered was that Amber liked him. Because of that, I wanted to like him, too, but I was also daddy's girl. I remember being so confused whenever she'd leave in tears after a fight with my parents. She loved Dylan, they blamed him for her changing, and that was all she wrote."

Cane stayed silent as she took a long pull of her beer, wanting to delay the rest of the story. Pretend it never happened. But it did, and it felt good to share it with someone who didn't know it already. Who hadn't already formed his own opinion based on town gossip, or even her own parents' testimonies.

Drawing a deep breath, Angelle blew it out slowly. She set down her drink, swallowed again, and said, "One night, Amber came home to babysit me. I was getting too old to need a sitter, but Daddy had a big fund-raiser and he was gonna be out all night. By that point, Amber had stopped bringing Dylan around with her on visits, so when she asked if I wanted to head to the city for dinner, I knew what was going on. We were meeting him, and even though breaking their rules made me nervous, I didn't want to disappoint her. So we went."

Angie closed her eyes as the pain of that night washed over her. "It was raining. Traffic lights were out, and it was taking longer than normal to get anywhere. I'm guessing Amber got impatient and floored it, I don't know. Mama always said she had a lead foot. All I remember is spinning. Spinning for what felt like forever. Really, it had to be only a few seconds. Then the screech of tires. A horn blaring. And glass shattering."

The car had flipped. She could still feel the cold, wet rain soaking her clothes. The panic of calling out for Amber and not getting a response sliced as raw and deep as it had seventeen years ago. A sob escaped, followed by another until her shoulders were shaking. She swiped at the tears falling down her cheeks and suddenly found herself yanked into Cane's rock hard chest. Her eyes flew open.

"I've got you."

Those words brought a fresh batch of waterworks. Gently,

he pried open the hand she'd clutched around the metal cap. She hadn't realized how tightly she was holding it. A red, angry spot marked her, and he pressed his lips softly against her skin. Tingles shot up her arm as he kicked the coffee table away and pulled her fully against him.

Leather, pine, and the soap from her parents' shower filled her head as Cane cradled her head in the crook of his neck. The soft cotton of his shirt grew damp from her tears. Angie closed her eyes as he tightened his hold, letting herself grieve for the sister she'd loved so much. The girl who was taken too young.

Cane seemed content just holding her, letting her cry it out. But she wanted him to know the rest of the story. So she drew a ragged wood-scented breath, trying to rein in her emotions.

"Amber"—Angelle hiccupped—"Amber died instantly. The impact of the flip trapped me in the back. I remember being scared. In pain and confused, but then thinking God had sent His angels to help." Sniffling, she raised her head and gave a watery grin. "Firefighters. They'd come to extract me from the car. It was terrifying, but they talked me through it. And then stayed until I went to the hospital. They saved me."

Cane brushed hair away from her face. "And now you're one of them."

She was. Pride at that accomplishment bloomed anew in her chest. It was all a part of her plan to become more than a timid, spineless mouse. For years she'd watched the men and women of the Bon Terre fire department from outside the library window. As a teen, she'd been a library aide and after college she returned to lead children's programming… all the while watching the heroic firefighters across the street. They lived their lives helping people, stepping outside of their comfort zones. There were times she'd been afraid of her own shadow. Always afraid of rocking the boat.

Angelle nodded and said, "Yeah, but you have to understand why that's so strange to people here." Not ready to leave the comfort of his arms, she shifted her weight onto his right thigh and leaned her back against the sofa cushions. "After Amber died, my parents went into lockdown mode. They blamed Dylan and her friends for the accident, and the little freedom I'd had before vanished completely. You've heard of helicopter parents? Well, mine were white-on-rice parents. I couldn't sneeze without having a wad of tissues thrust under my nose or get a chill without being thrown a blanket. But I understood. I got it. They were older and hurting, and I didn't want to do anything to make it worse. So I fell in line. I did what was expected, and faded into the shadows."

"Until this year," Cane guessed, glancing at the wrist cradled between them. "Tell me about your tattoo. What does it mean to you?"

Shoulders back, tears abated, she told him, "It means I'm starting over. The faded line down the middle is a scar from the accident. It symbolizes when my life changed and I turned to fear, and I wanted to replace it with the opposite. Amber hadn't been afraid to take chances, to try something different with her life and find her own path. That's what I want. The artist warned me it wouldn't totally cover my scar—the line shows in the negative space between the letters. But I didn't need it covered completely. This shaped me. And really, I couldn't ask for anything better." Glancing at the inked promise she'd made to herself, she laughed at the result. "This tattoo perfectly reflects who I am. A woman striving to be bold and transformed, but with hints of her past always shining through."

Cane's body shifted beneath her and she raised her head. That fire was back, along with what appeared to be respect. He shook his head and said, "You don't give yourself enough credit. The woman I know *is* bold. Darlin', starting over is scary as shit. You left a town where everyone knew you and moved where no one did. You went after the career you wanted, and now you're a hero. You're a woman in a man's job, and in a position to help someone trapped like you were. You rush into burning buildings to save lives, and yesterday when you faced the firing squad of your own family, you did it with class. When they judged, you smiled but you didn't make excuses or apologize for your choices. That's brave. No, scratch that. It's badass."

Angelle laughed, thinking, *That's me, all right. One fierce chica.* But then a wicked gleam entered Cane's eyes and with his gaze locked on hers, he lifted her wrist to his mouth. Electricity zinged through her veins as he pressed a kiss across her skin. Right over the word *Chance.* Then, a glint entered his eye as he slid up and took her thumb into his hot mouth. The world dropped away.

It was a sign. A sign from the cosmos, the heavens, or maybe just Amber. This right here, this man, was the ultimate chance Angelle would ever get.

"Badass?" she asked, hearing how breathless her voice suddenly sounded but not giving a hoot. "I like the sound of that." Then shifting her weight, she straddled Cane Robicheaux, grabbed either side of his dark head, stared into his widened, hungry eyes, and kissed him.

Chapter Ten

The sound of female voices roused Cane from his sleep. He'd been dreaming of Angelle, his subconscious filling in what could have happened had Troy and Eva not come home so early. It was probably for the best. Sadie had been sleeping down the hall, and their first time was not gonna be a rush job on the floor of her brother's house. No, Cane planned to take his time. To explore and appreciate and *memorize* every inch of Angelle's creamy white skin. After that, then they'd have time for fast and furious on the carpet.

That thought was enough to wake his ass up for good.

Thanksgiving Day in the Robicheaux family usually involved his dad deep-frying a turkey, Sherry bringing a pathetic looking yet delicious apple pie, and Cane making most of the sides. He'd inherited the job when his mom died, but with Colby back, maybe she'd take over that load. After throwing on a pair of jeans and a button-down, he texted Sherry about the mirliton casserole he'd left in the freezer. Then, with Angelle's suggestion for him to sleep late fresh in his mind, and the lack of any male voices from down the hall,

Cane cracked open his dog-eared copy of *Freakonomics*.

Halfway through a chapter on what makes a perfect parent—clearly not his own—the scent of strong brewed coffee and sweet homemade bread beckoned from the kitchen. Clearly, it was time to join the land of the living.

"Now the whole parade is in jeopardy," Angelle's mom was saying as he entered the crowded room. The women had gathered around the large island, Mrs. Prejean, Angelle, Lacey, Eva, and Ryan's wife, Tonya. His hostess's back was to him as she leaned over to check the ham in the oven. "It's not Bubba's fault he has appendicitis, of course, but I don't know what we're gonna do."

Lacey and Eva smiled in greeting when they saw him at the door, and Tonya nodded. It appeared she was still a Brady holdout. Nodding back with the grin that usually won him favors, Cane stopped by the coffee pot that had been calling his name. Winning over family required his morning jolt of caffeine.

Angelle strolled over, an adorable wrinkle on her forehead. Her fingertips brushed the side of her face before reaching inside the cabinet, and Cane remembered his reading glasses.

"Guess the cat's out of the bag," he said, peering at her from beneath his wire frames. "I'm a closet nerd."

"I think it's rather sexy," she replied, her sultry voice lowered to a whisper. Her shy smile and the pink in her cheeks implied her declaration surprised her as much as it had him. Handing over a mug emblazoned with a turkey wearing overalls, she smiled at the ground and said, "Good morning."

He grinned as his hand enveloped hers around the ceramic. "It is now."

It was a cliché, but damn if it wasn't the truth. She was adorable, and in her festive green skirt, white blouse, and flour-dusted apron, the woman looked good enough to eat.

His arms twitched to hold her again, and a sudden surge of want shot through him. Want, backed by an emotion that sent his pulse racing.

Cane took a quick step back, breaking the contact.

Turning from her questioning gaze, he took his mug and filled it to the brim. *It's just a lingering memory of the dream.* Between that and this whole hoax they had going, his mind and body were getting jumbled. Not about wanting her—that was a given. But whatever this was between them, it could only ever be physical. There was no room for confusion on that point.

When he turned back, a frown line marred the soft skin between her eyebrows. Needing a distraction, Cane palmed his mug and blew over the top. "What's in jeopardy?"

As distractions went, it was a good one. Or a bad one, depending on your viewpoint. Every female eye in the room zeroed in on him, and they all began talking at once. Sipping his coffee, Cane listened, mildly overwhelmed, as they explained the annual Christmas parade, how important it was to the town, and how their *Papa Noel* had just been carted to the hospital.

When they finished, Cane glanced down at Angelle. "Papa Noel? Is this another *country* Cajun thing?"

The look of hurt and uncertainty long gone, erased by worry over her beloved parade, she explained. "Santa Claus. He rides in the last float, waves and *ho-ho-ho*s, and tosses treats to all the kids. It's the highlight of the whole thing, and Papa and Daddy already have roles. So do Troy and Ryan. Everyone does. This parade is planned like a year in advance, and right now we're short one jolly fat guy."

Cane couldn't believe where his thoughts were going or the words tickling his tongue. But staring into Angelle's sad green eyes turned him into a puddle of sap. Her mouth was meant for smiling, and that's what prompted him to say, "I take it there's a suit I could borrow?"

It took about a second longer than he thought, but then there it was. Perfection. The smile built slowly until it nearly took over her face, and it was like taking a sucker punch to the gut in one of his classes at the gym. For a smile like that, Cane was willing to do just about anything. And apparently, he was about to prove it.

• • •

A soft chuckle pulled Cane's attention away from his plate. Thanksgiving dinner was half over. He'd lost count of the number of people there, but it had to be pushing fifty. Tables were shoved together throughout the wide living room and kitchen, where every Cajun dish he could think of was present. The huge ham that'd been tempting him all morning was joined by a pork *and* beef roast, both smothered with gravy, candied yams, jambalaya, rice and gravy, gumbo, and a dish Cane had never heard of, corn maque choux. He didn't know what it was, but it was freaking delicious.

As one of Angelle's many cousins said while filling his plate, "If you leave here hungry, it's your own damn fault."

Glancing over at his giggling fiancée, he wiped his mouth on a napkin and asked, "What's so funny?"

"You only eat one thing at a time." She pointed her fork at what was left of his meal, green eyes dancing with amusement. "You did it last night, too. Is there a method to your culinary madness, or are you just in the food zone?"

Cane leaned back in his metal chair, thoughts of finishing his jambalaya abandoned. Confident and teasing were definitely his two favorite hellcat traits. "I'll have you know that some believe eating this way is better for the body," he informed her, fully aware that his nerd flag was flying and not giving a damn. "Foods break down differently, and eating one thing at a time can ease digestion. It's also said that people who do it are more task-oriented."

"More like inflexible and stubborn," Angelle muttered with a smirk. "And what about people who mix it up and inhale their food, like yours truly? Got an answer for that?"

She batted her eyelashes, clearly believing she'd stumped him, which made it all the more gratifying when he replied, "Fast eating is linked with putting others first. As for mixing it up, they *say* it implies you're great at handling responsibility." He grinned and added, "Personally, I think it means you eat weird."

Angelle shook her head and narrowed her inquisitive eyes, looking as if she'd never seen him before. And in a way, she hadn't. After a moment of shocked silence, she recovered and asked, "Do you, like, memorize Wikipedia for fun?"

More like Discovery Channel. Cane shrugged. "I like to be informed."

She smiled, a soft natural smile seemingly meant for him and not for show. Even as euphoria hit his blood, seeing that directed at him instead of the fearful looks she used to give him, anxiety knotted his stomach. She was getting attached.

Close friendship was good. Or so he thought, having never had that before. Seeing another man take her home and make her smile would kill him—but it would be for the best. And at least those honest smiles, that feisty spunk, and the scent of sunflowers would remain in his life. But she had to know it could never be anything more.

"Speaking of informed." Her cousin Lacey's voice broke from across the table, snapping both their heads forward. Suspicion lit her hazel eyes and had her tapping a painted nail on the tabletop. "How does one's fiancée not notice that kind of food quirk before?"

Nails bit into the denim on his thigh. The art of lying— on the spot or otherwise—was not one of Angelle's gifts.

Cane hated dishonesty, too, but a life of smoke and mirrors had unfortunately honed a talent. Taking her small hand in his, he shrugged again, this time in a confident display of nonchalance. *Never let them see you sweat* was rule one.

"I've been this way all my life," he said, leaning back and leisurely lifting his mouth in a grin. *Distraction by charm* was rule two. "But you'd be surprised how long it takes some people to notice. Your cousin must've been too busy staring at this sexy mug of mine to notice my eating habits."

The double eye-roll from both women was almost audible—but the trick worked. Only a trace of doubt lingered in Lacey's voice as she replied, "Good Lord, it's a miracle that head of yours fits through the door," and Angelle slumped beside him.

Another disaster averted.

His fiancée for the week resumed eating as the *ding* of silver on crystal filled the room. Mrs. Prejean stood from her position of honor near the head of the table and gazed over her gathered friends and family. Raising her wineglass, her mouth curved in a smile much like her daughter's. "It's about that time," she said, smile widening as playful groans erupted. Talking over them she said, "Y'all hush now. This is my favorite part. I have a lot to be thankful for this year. My family is together again, we're adding to our numbers, and talented hands helped prepare a delicious supper. Ladies, you outdid yourselves."

Cane joined the chorus of *hear hear*s. The food was phenomenal. The new hole in his belt proved he'd be hitting the gym hard when they got back, but it had been worth every bite.

"I have one final gratitude today, a surprising one born from a sad circumstance." Whispers sprang up among the folding tables covered with red plastic, and Mrs. Prejean caught his eye and winked. "As you all know, poor Bubba's appendicitis left our parade in a real bind. The children need a Santa Claus. But I'm very happy to say my future son-in-law has stepped up to fill his shoes. Bon Terre, meet this year's Papa Noel!"

Whispers turned to applause as the attention shifted in Cane's direction. Guarded glances transformed into approval for the first time since he'd arrived. Technically, he knew it shouldn't matter. But as he glanced at the generations gathered around, Cane couldn't deny a sense of satisfaction.

The only person he'd done it for was sitting beside him. But accepting him meant accepting Angelle's choices. More than that, he genuinely liked these people. He had his sisters, whom he loved more than life, and he had Jason and Emma… but that was it. Most families in New Orleans were huge. The product of only children, he was the last to carry on the Robicheaux name. He'd never known what it was like to have a big family. Now that he'd gotten a glimpse, he saw what he'd been missing. Angelle squeezed his thigh, and he sent her a wink. This was nice.

Then, her dad stood up. "If I may say a few words." All those good feelings obliterated.

Hearing about the circumstances around Amber's death put a lot of things in perspective. Cane thought it was small-minded to judge a man based on tattoos, piercings, or any of the exterior things—but then, he'd used some of those very things to *keep* people at a distance. Knowing people would judge him, just as Angelle's father had done. And with what the man had gone through, Cane couldn't blame him.

It didn't make listening to whatever he was about to say any easier.

The older man inhaled deeply as he looked about the room. "Thanksgiving is a time we remember family," he said, voice strong and clear. Every bit a town mayor. "Loved ones. People we have lost and those who've recently come into our acquaintance. Amber is with us today, and though her time on earth was short, I'm grateful for the years we did have her, and I feel good knowing she's now a guardian angel, looking out for us."

Angelle exhaled a broken breath and Cane slid his arm behind her chair. Her father's eyes shifted and came to rest on Cane. "This year, the good Lord brought my daughter's fiancé into our lives. A city boy from *Nawlins*," he teased with a smile, making the entire room, Cane included, chuckle. "At first, I didn't much know how to take him. To be honest, he didn't seem right for my little girl. But I've been watching. Him stepping up for the parade speaks to his character. So does the tenderness he shows my daughter. And the fact that she lights up like a Christmas Eve bonfire whenever he enters a room proves he makes her happy."

Guilt walloped Cane in the chest. The stiffening of Angelle's shoulders said she felt the same thing. She closed her eyes as her teeth sank into her lip, and Cane glanced back to see the mayor walk over and hold out his hand. "As long as you keep making her happy, you two have my blessing."

Cane stared at the outstretched hand. This was what they'd wanted. Her family believed their story. But getting her father's blessing, knowing it was hard earned and sincere, hit harder than Cane would've ever expected. With the room watching, and as Angelle wiped at the tear falling down her cheek, he shook the man's hand and spoke around a slightly thickened throat. "Thank you."

Still clutching his hand, her father turned to address the room again. "Now, tomorrow's the big Cracklin Cook-Off. I'm thinking we teach my city boy future son-in-law how it's really done. Should we let Cane join the Ragin' Cajun Prejean Mafia?"

Cheers and *whoop*s met the question, and Cane looked to Angelle for help. Closing her shocked open mouth, she cleared her throat and explained, "The Mafia is Daddy's cooking team. It's a big deal; they've won the last four years counting." She licked her lips and gave him a pained smile. "It's always *only* been family. Daddy, Ryan, and Troy."

Meaning Brady had never been invited.

That wasn't what Cane should focus on, but damn if he could help it. Oh, the guilt over the hoax was still there—in fact, he got an extra dose with the older man's request. But it also brought a ridiculous sense of triumph.

They were already in the thick of it. He might as well keep it up, especially since it was getting Angelle what she wanted. He was curious about this *Ragin' Cajun* life he'd gotten to see, and he wanted to know more. Besides, he couldn't very well say no. With a grateful smile, he replied, "It'd be an honor."

Smiling, the old man clapped him on the shoulder. "Welcome to the family, son. You keep my little girl safe and happy, you hear?"

Safe and happy.

Cane looked at the woman beside him, her green eyes still conflicted over this latest development. But happiness was also there. Affection, too. And as her gaze slid across his face, Cane thought he saw a glimmer of hope. Of wanting more than he could ever give. That was enough to douse any sense of victory or satisfaction.

"You have my word," he promised. He'd keep her safe, all right.

Even from himself.

Chapter Eleven

Eating crow.

That's what the good people of Bon Terre were doing as Angelle and Cane strolled through Les Acadiens Park that morning. Word had spread like wildfire about the city boy Papa Noel, and the mayor bestowing his seal of approval on the match. That'd been enough to transform the cold, aloof acquaintances from the *boucherie* into sweet-smiling friends issuing invites to dinner.

The abrupt change had *almost* made Angelle laugh.

What kept her from doing so had been the lingering blanket of guilt for deceiving her family. All she'd hoped to prove was that they didn't need to worry about her. That she was doing just fine on her own and had moved on from Brady. Well, mission accomplished, message received. The problem was, now she had to deal with the fallout of her lie. But honestly, she didn't know which was worse: letting her loved ones needlessly worry, or harmlessly pretending a romance to spare their feelings.

Especially when said romance *wasn't* completely pretend.

At least not anymore.

Angie's poor heart was in a galactic game of tug-of-war. The man her family was beginning to care for was the same man who'd been shocking the heck out of her since they'd arrived. Brain-scrambling kisses aside, Cane Robicheaux was a child-whispering, factoid-spouting, sister-protecting, amazing-smelling (a trait that cannot be left out) hunk of swoon-worthy material. Every instinct she had screamed that she'd pegged him all wrong, and that she needed to latch on, good and tight, before another woman swooped in and snagged him.

"What you all smiling about?" Lacey asked, coming up behind her to fluff Angie's hair. "No tears for passing over your crown today?"

Angie snorted. "Are you kidding me? Though it's been an honor, I'm happy to hand over my reign as Queen of Fried Pig Fat. Let someone else gain ten pounds today."

Lacey made a face at the brown paper bag in her hand. Tilting her head, she pursed her lips as if pondering, then shrugged, shoved her hand inside, and drew out two thick pieces, popping them in her mouth with a wink. "As happy as you sound," she said through a startlingly full mouth, "something tells me that smile still had more to do with a certain leather-wearing hottie than your cracklin title."

Lacey swung her gaze over to the Ragin' Cajun Prejean Mafia pop-up tent. It stood at the end of a long line of similar ones, only theirs was deep red with gold flames and had a boiling pig in the center. It was bright, bold, and to tell the truth, an eyesore. But in some crazed, whacked-out way, it represented her family.

Cane was easy to spot inside the tent. The leather jacket was gone. So were the sneakers. But he still stood out. Maybe because he was taller than any of the men in her family, or it was the air of confidence he exuded. Maybe her body was simply attuned to his. But whatever the reason, the moment her gaze fell on his strong profile clenched in effort, the sounds around her seemed to mute.

Soft black cotton strained as Cane stirred the contents of a cast iron pot with a long metal pole. Troy and Ryan stood to the side, beers in hand, talking animatedly. Cane nodded and laughed, and her pulse went wonky.

He'd actually done it. Somewhere between being so good with Sadie, stepping up as Papa Noel, earning Daddy's acceptance, and cooking out today, Cane had won over her impossibly overbearing big brother. Watching Troy slap Cane on the shoulder toppled any remaining barriers Angelle might've had. And when her fake fiancé's face lit up in a returning smile, that wonky pulse of hers skipped a beat.

This was no game. In this moment, she knew Cane wasn't acting. He was being real, being *him*, and fitting into her life, her family, so easily it was like he was meant to be there. When they'd left that morning, Angelle could tell Cane felt honored to be included. And he should. She hadn't been lying when she'd said it had only ever been family. Brady had never *quite* made it to that status. It'd been a long-standing joke for years, that he'd have to bide his time in his own family's second-place tent until their engagement became *official*. That day never came.

Perhaps reading her thoughts, Lacey said, "You know, Red, I love Brady. He's a great guy, and a good friend. But I never really saw the two of you lasting."

Color Angelle surprised. She'd figured the whole town, at the very least her entire family, had been waving the Brady and Angelle Golden Couple banner for years. "You didn't?"

"Nope. There was no heat. No spark." Lacey scuffed her boot along the ground, looking thoughtful. "You two were sweet, and I could tell you cared a lot about him. But you know how they say one person in a relationship is always the reacher? That they care a little more, hope a little harder?"

Angie made a face, knowing where this was going. She'd never felt quite good enough for the "good doctor," but she certainly didn't need her own blood confirming it. Still, she said, "Yeah?"

Lacey shrugged. "That was Brady."

Eyes wide, Angelle propped her hip on a folding table and sputtered, "Say what?"

"I speak the God's truth," her cousin declared. "He was gone a lot with school, and maybe that's why. But whenever he *was* home, it was obvious your heart wasn't in it. At least to me." She hitched her thumb over her shoulder, back in the direction of the Ragin Cajun tent. "But with *that* man over there? Opposites must attract because there's so much sparkage, you two should walk around with a warning label. *Caution: Couple may burst into flame at a moment's notice.*"

Angelle rolled her eyes and ducked her head, pretending to adjust her Cracklin Queen sash over her simple blouse and jeans. Warmth flooded her cheeks, but inwardly she was pleased as pie. It hadn't just been her imagination or wishful thinking. She and Cane had heat. Serious heat. And he genuinely seemed to care about her.

Lacey pushed up on the table and slid her arm around Angie's shoulders. "From where I sit, y'all seem evenly matched. I'm happy for you, Little Red. And a bit jealous."

Giddiness bloomed at her cousin's confirmation.

Then Lacey added, "Fake engagement or not, you two are perfect for each other."

Giddiness that turned to shock. "Wh-*what*?"

Lacey chuckled. "C'mon, Red. Did you honestly think you could pull a fast one on the town sneak? I know you too well. Plus, those blushes and stammers are dead giveaways."

Angelle's gaze darted back to the pop-up tent, straining to see her family's expressions. Was this all a set-up? Were they about to be busted, in front of the whole of Bon Terre?

"Don't worry," Lacey said, reading her thoughts. "Your secret's safe with me. No one else suspects from what I can tell. I just wanted you to know that *I* know, and that I'm on your side."

It was like old times, the two of them with a secret. Many a scrape had been caused *and* avoided by them pairing up — the only difference was now *petite fille* was in the driver's seat.

Pressing a kiss on top of Angelle's head, Lacey swung her foot. "Magnolia Springs has done you good, girl. You're finally going after what you want, taking control. Taking chances," she added, wrapping her finger and thumb around Angie's wrist. "I don't know what game you thought you were running coming here, but I can tell you what's happening. You've got this town talking. Seeing you different. You're confident and strong, and I'm proud as hell. As for the yummy man-candy, you've convinced the family he's yours. Now it's time he knew, too."

As Lacey squeezed her tighter, the bottle cap dug into her thigh. It hadn't left her pocket since her babysitting jaunt with Cane. She'd unfortunately misplaced the second one, which made this cap even more special. It was a memento of the night she'd bared her soul to a playboy and received more love and understanding *and desire* than she could've ever imagined.

The night, she may as well admit now, she'd begun falling in love with her fake fiancé.

• • •

After a long and very interesting morning, Cane could proudly claim he'd graduated from a cracklin novice. He was no expert, but he'd learned the difference between pork rinds and a true cracklin (the first is just fat, as opposed to chunks of pork fat, skin, and meat), and he'd held his own during the frying. In fact, the only stumble Cane had all morning didn't even come until the judges had stopped by for a sample.

Standing around, waiting to see who'd won the amateur category, Angelle's dad greeted him with a beer. "Got a second to talk, son?"

Cane was no chump, but the man intimidated him. Years of being in government had clearly given him a low bullshit tolerance, and while Cane hated bullshit…well, he sure was selling a lot of it this week.

Accepting the beer, having a feeling he was going to need it, he said, "Sure, Mr. Prejean."

"Call me David." The man took a pull of his beer, eyes trained on the passing crowd. "I realize things may be different in the city, but down here, a man asks a father's permission to marry his daughter."

Shit. Cane popped the top on his beer and chugged. Honestly, contrary to popular belief, things weren't that different where he grew up. If Cane were ever to propose for real—though that would never happen—he would definitely ask the woman's father first. It was tradition and showed respect. But this *wasn't* real. The words *will you marry me* never left his mouth once. Nor would they ever, to anyone.

But Cane couldn't tell her father that. Not without pulling the plug on the whole deal. Which meant he had to stand there and take his lumps, apologizing for the one crime out of the entire hoax he hadn't actually committed. Awesome.

With a chokehold of guilt cutting off his air supply, Cane inhaled a breath, preparing to lie solo. To the man who'd opened his home and family to him, no less. Neck muscles straining, he turned to David and said, "You're right. It was disrespectful. And I have no excuse other than we got caught up in the moment."

Over her father's shoulder, Cane locked eyes with Angelle

across the crowded field. Looking at her somehow made the deceit easier. "Your daughter is a remarkable woman. I'm sure you know that. She's beautiful and strong. Has a heart bigger than anyone I've ever met, and is hilarious without even trying to be. She's a total klutz and makes a drunkard look graceful, but she's adorable and kind and perfect." Even though she couldn't hear their conversation, Angelle's face pulled into a wide, dazzling smile, and as the force of it hit him in the chest, Cane said, "It's impossible not to want to be near her as much as possible. To keep that smile pointed at you. Forever if you could."

Every word he'd said was the truth. And that scared the shit out of him.

The line had shifted. The green eyes drilling into his now spoke of more than just a game. More than an affair. Emotions that, if he wasn't careful, could lead to love. Looking away from the woman burrowing deep inside his head, Cane looked at David. The man's smile, while not as wide or as dazzling, spoke volumes. He'd been forgiven for not following protocol. That forgiveness probably wouldn't extend to his real sins, though.

A screech of feedback preceded a man's voice calling for the contestants in the amateur's division. Angelle's father lifted his chin and said, "I'm glad we had this talk. Now, what do you say we go get that trophy?"

Cane nodded and followed the man to the stage, chugging his beer along the way. It was Friday. Just three more days and then they'd leave for home. Cane was glad he'd come, he'd enjoyed getting to know this town and these people, and he'd never regret spending time with Angelle. But he was getting in too deep. It was starting to become all too real. And that was dangerous.

The three former Cracklin Queens—Sadie, Angelle, and a woman with gray hair piled high on her head and a beer in one hand—stood near the microphone, ready to give the awards. The announcer, a man who'd introduced himself as T-Bob, consulted his clipboard before saying, "Today's contest was a good one. The judges informed me it was the closest they'd seen in years."

Great. The one year Cane joined the Mafia, other teams decided to step up their game. If they lost today, even though he'd done very little of the work, it would appear to be his fault. As if by joining the team, he'd cursed them with—what had the guys called it the other night when they were playing cards? Cane grinned as the word came to him. The *gris gris*.

Brady stood with his father and brother just a few feet away, and the men locked eyes. His smile faded.

"In third place, with a *very* respectable showing and tasty treat…the Verret family!"

The crowd cheered as one of the few family teams that included children stepped forward. Along with the trophy, the elder queen bestowed a foam pig crown on each of their heads. The young girl who reminded Cane of Emma made a face and quickly took hers off.

"First place and second place had a very slim margin, and that's why it took longer than normal to reach a decision. Nevertheless, we've reached consensus, and our second place winners should be very proud of themselves. Come on up here…Doucet family!"

Cane exhaled, relieved, as Brady and his dad stepped forward. Before walking to the stage, they sauntered over to the Mafia. "One day, my boys and I are gonna get you, David. Mark my words now."

He stood stone-faced for a second before bursting into deep laughter. All the men joined in, shaking hands, clearly taking the contest in stride. And then Brady stopped in front of Cane.

"Good job out there," he said, pumping his hand once.

He looked as uncomfortable as Cane felt.

"Yeah, you, too," Cane replied, not knowing if that was remotely true. He hadn't sampled the other team's offerings nor watched them work. He hadn't wanted to seem as though he was gloating over being on the Mafia, though secretly he kind of was.

The men received their trophy, and then Sadie tapped a plump finger against her mouth as she looked at the tall men. Glancing at the crowns before her, she requested in a loud voice, "Put me on the table!" From her now considerable height, she was able to put the crowns on their heads, giggling as Brady tweaked her nose. The reminder of his closeness to Angelle's family rattled. But the jealousy annoyed even more. *Three more days.*

"And I guess y'all know what's coming," the announcer teased, earning a laugh from the crowd. "Looks like the streak is still alive! Come on up here, Prejean Mafia, and get your trophy. You know the drill by now."

Head held high—as if anything he'd done actually won them first place—Cane followed Angelle's father and brothers onto the stage. Angelle stepped forward, handing the huge trophy over to her dad and wrapping him in a hug. Then she set the foam crowns on her brothers' heads, placing a kiss on each of their cheeks.

Cane grinned as she stopped in front of him. Pointing to his stubbled cheek, he leaned forward and said, "Got one of those for me, darlin'?"

Angelle bit her lip and shook her head. "No." Eyes dancing, she set the crown on his head and palmed both sides of his face. Pulling him in close, she said against his mouth, "I've got something better." Then, with the sound of her words echoing over the speaker, and the crowd hooting their approval, she planted a big wet one on his lips.

Chapter Twelve

Cracklin Queen no more, Angelle was free to enjoy the rest of the festival as a civilian. And enjoy it she did. She'd dragged Cane on all of her favorite rides, cuddling on the Ferris wheel, stifling a laugh as he got dizzy on the Tilt-a-Whirl, and they'd devoured snacks from the best stands. Now, one hand around the large pink and black zebra Cane had won for her, Angie tapped her toe to the beat of the Bergeron Heartbreakers.

"You like dancing, don't you?"

Smiling, she looked at Cane and said, "All-city champ senior year of high school, and a blue ribbon repeat. Brady and I used to compete together. Going to competitions was one of the few ways I knew I'd definitely see him once he went off to school."

A strange expression washed over Cane's face and he glanced at the dance floor. Nodding subtly, as if talking to himself, he turned back and said, "Teach me?"

Excitement bubbled in her tummy, spreading through her veins. She loved dancing, but more than that, she *loved* being in Cane's arms. She bit her lip as he held out his hand and she placed hers in it. Warmth enveloped her skin, stirring up the blood until she was sure her pulse matched the upbeat tempo. "Just don't step on my feet, city boy."

At the edge of the dance floor, Angelle found them a spot a little ways from the crowd. Cajun dancing could be as easy or as complicated as you wanted to make it. As a beginner, one who had a heck of a lot of pride, she figured she'd go light on Cane. Especially since people were already eyeing them with curiosity.

"Okay, so we'll start with the open-handed position," she told him. "From here, we can do several easy moves you've probably seen before. You'll look like a pro in no time."

He chuckled as if he doubted it, but she ignored him. With two older brothers, she'd seen enough macho behavior to last her a lifetime. Cane was worried about failing—whether it was because he didn't want to look stupid in front of the town or her, she didn't know. But it didn't matter, either, because what he failed to realize was that Angie was a damn fine teacher.

"Now, old-school dancing is a bit different, but with the Cajun swing and Zydeco, you want rhythm. Your body should be fluid and bop to the beat." Elbows bent and close to her sides, she took his hands and swung them along with the tempo. He raised an eyebrow, and she rolled her eyes. "You're a musician, so don't even tell me you can't find the beat."

Cane chuckled and then swung his arms, flawlessly finding the rhythm. They added the feet, pumping with a bounce step, and the amused lightness on his face filled her with so much happiness she thought she'd burst. For a time, Cajun dancing had defined her. The dance floor had been the one place she let herself go, where she didn't care who her family was or what people expected of her. She lost herself in the lively music and the fast-paced steps. And now, she was sharing it with Cane.

This was the icing on the cake of an already perfect day.

Once the basic step was solid, Angelle quickly taught
Cane key moves like the Sweetheart, the Hip Turn, and the
Turn-Under. And after several minutes of practice, delightful
moments filled with missteps, laughter, and a whole lot of
tingles, Angie declared him ready for his dance floor debut.

"If it makes you happy, angel, I'll do just about anything.
I believe I owe you a date from the auction." Cane looked
to the crowd of colorfully dressed couples spinning, shuffling,
and sliding along the plywood. "But you have to know I'm
gonna be a bull in a china shop out there."

"No, you won't." While it was true they wouldn't be
winning any dance awards tonight, after only a few songs,
Cane was really doing well. "And yes, it *would* make me
happy."

She smiled brightly, feeling a strange surge of confidence.
Cane's gaze glided over her face, a grin pulling at his mouth,
and he pressed a soft kiss on the tip of her nose. "Then lead
on, tiny dancer," he said, his voice teasing.

Hand in hand, still smiling, they walked out onto the
true dance floor. Men and women she'd known all her life
winked as they glided past, and Angelle knew what they were
thinking. *A young couple in love.* Angie bit her lip when they
reached the center.

Grinning mischievously, Cane took her hands in his. And
then, they began to dance.

As they swirled around the floor, Angie felt like she was
in a movie. A movie that actually showed Cajun people right,
instead of a bunch of toothless twits like on *Waterboy*. They
weren't perfect. Cane still stumbled and got confused. One
time, he even stepped on her toes. But it was in those mistakes
that Angelle lost a bit more of her heart. He was trying, trying
for *her,* and he was there, for *her.* The sexy, intelligent, witty
playboy before her was willing to make an ass out of himself
for the sake of the cause…and because it made her happy.

That was worth more than a bazillion blue ribbons and championships.

When the song ended, Cane pulled her close, wrapping his arms around her. Leather, woodsy cologne, and yummy man filled her head, as his pulse beat against her cheek.

"That was fun," he said into her hair. He kissed the top of her head, but he didn't move. He seemed perfectly content just to hold her, standing stock still in the middle of the dance floor. And Angelle had zero complaints.

The band announced they were taking a break, and a familiar country tune played through the speakers. Cane leaned back, skimmed his fingers down her arms until he met her hands, and said, "How about we dance this one *my* way?"

His voice was low and seductive, like the notes of the song. The way the sound affected her, Angie was sure she'd have agreed to anything, which was good, since Cane didn't wait for her permission.

Gaze locked on hers, he walked backward, pulling her out of the way of the other couples. Along the edge, with shadows flickering over his face, Cane slid one of her arms around his neck, and then the other, before slipping his own around her waist. Then, holding her firmly against him, he began to move.

And oh, how he *moved*.

This wasn't Cajun dancing. Angelle wasn't sure this could be called dancing at all. But it was the sexiest thing she'd ever done. The way he held her in his arms, gently, like she was precious, yet tightly, like he never wanted to let her go, had her heart in her throat. The feel of his hips swiveling and brushing against hers sent shivers skating over her body. And the way his eyes didn't stray once left Angie feeling he could see straight to her soul.

Dancing with Brady had never felt like this. With him, the most she'd ever felt was warm and safe. Comfortable. Not as if she could go up in flames at any moment. That was how she knew with every zinging nerve in her body that she'd been right earlier—she was falling for this surprising man.

After months of fighting the tension snapping between them, one week alone with Cane put the beat down on every single one of her defenses. His reputation, her prejudices, and the worry over her heart. That ship had sailed. She'd fallen for her own lie. Now, there was only one thing left to do.

Okay, there were several things left to do, but *one* held very high priority for her tonight.

"You know, you really shouldn't look at me like that." Cane's rough voice sent a fresh shot of electricity down her spine, straight into her toes.

"And how am I looking at you?" she asked, knowing full well, but wanting to hear him say it.

"Like you want me to wrap those pretty little legs around my waist and haul you out to my truck." His mouth twitched as if he was trying to make a joke, but his heavy-lidded eyes were almost black, and his voice had grown deeper. More rough. Clearing it, he said, "And you shouldn't look at me like that unless you're willing to act on it."

Angelle's stomach bottomed out. Her breathing stuttered.

This was her moment.

A choice between finally taking a real chance or turning tail and running. The next words out of her mouth would determine if she was ready to embrace the woman she *wanted* to be or if she'd fall back into the same old trap that had held her for years. *Fear.*

No virgin in her right mind wouldn't be at least a *little* scared in this situation. Cane Robicheaux wasn't just experienced—if talk held true, he'd practically written the book on how to pleasure a woman. But her cousin had been right: she wasn't the same girl anymore. She'd finally gone after the career she'd always wanted. She'd sought out the freedom she'd craved. And now was her chance to prove just how audacious she'd become.

Exhaling long and slow, she raised her head and said, "Maybe I'm more than willing."

He froze. Just stopped dancing, right on the shadowed edge of the floor.

Cane stared at her, looking deep into her eyes as if searching for the punch line. But she wasn't joking. Angelle looked back confidently, willing him to see the truth. Well, maybe not the whole truth. She'd eventually have to mention the small fact that this time would be her *first* time, but she was aiming for that to be a heat-of-the-moment type of confession.

The slow song ended, replaced by a faster one. Couples simply danced around them, chuckling at the duo locked in an eye war on the dance floor. Until finally, thankfully, that sexy smile began curling Cane's mouth. And when the dimple appeared, the sight that always hit her smack in the chest, the hallelujah chorus echoed in her head.

This was happening. This was really, truly, going to happen. *Oh, crap.*

Just like that, Angie's good friends the horseflies came back, only this time they partnered with a flock of buzzards to dance the two-step in her tummy. This wasn't a simple case of nerves. This went beyond that. It went beyond performance anxiety, too. But as she looked into Cane's handsome face, soaked in the warmth of the smile just for her, Angelle knew the reward would be worth it.

"Mind if I cut in?"

Angelle blinked out of her Cane-coma and discovered Brady, smiling awkwardly with his hands in his pockets in front of them. She wondered how long he'd been standing there.

"Angie and I used to be partners," he said, glancing at Cane. "And it's been awhile since we danced. I'd hope that after all this, we can still be friends." Brady shrugged. "Friends dance, right?"

Angelle felt Cane's heated stare like a brand on her skin. With a slow nod, he said, "Sure. Friends dance." He glanced to the side, jaw flexing as he did. "But I'm gonna need a minute before I'm willing to let her go."

Brady's mouth tightened. "I'll just go grab a beer." He transferred his gaze to her and said, "I'll be right back."

His face was serious, attention laser-focused, but she simply nodded, already following Cane as he walked farther into the shadows. He ducked behind a post and drew her into his arms. She grinned. Anyone who would've been watching would know what he was doing. Cane was staking his claim. It wasn't blatant; any onlooker would have to go out of their way to watch. But it was a message. A clear one.

And what a lovely message it is.

Excitement snapped under her skin as Cane's head descended. A voice whispered, *is this just for show?* But Angelle ignored it, eager for another one of his kisses. The last thing Angelle saw before she closed her eyes was a fierce look masking his features…then his mouth touched hers, and she was lost.

Cane's mouth was heaven and hell rolled into one. A delicious torment she never wanted to end. The firm pressure mixed with the soft, skillful nibbles made her head spin. His tongue dipped inside as his long fingers raked over her back. Every muscle he touched sang under the glorious pressure, even as her lower half clenched, wanting more.

Mini-explosions went off in her insides. Nerves pulsed. Shockwaves reverberated down to her toes. Body parts that had laid dormant for twenty-six years sprang to life. A sound between a squeal and a groan left her mouth, and a rumble emanated from within Cane's chest. She was like a blazing sign saying, *take me now,* and the beautiful thing was, he would be doing just that, very soon.

Even as she thought it, fear crept in, but she whisked that away. She had plenty of time for that later. Right now, she wanted to focus on the crazy sensations coursing through her body. Cane's mouth curved in a smile as his hands cupped her backside and yanked her roughly against him. *Oh my*. The gesture was dominant, possessive. But she loved it.

Because tonight she *would* be his.

She whimpered when he tore his mouth away, pressing his forehead against hers. Ragged breath hit her lips as his hooded eyes penetrated hers.

"Go have your fun with Brady," he told her, fingers brushing her hair away from her face. She was positive it was knotted and standing on end, but she didn't give a damn. It was worth it. "You two give the people a show. But while you're in his arms on the dance floor, remember whose arms you're gonna be in tonight."

Cane kissed her again, hard and hungry—*passionately*— and when she went to cling to his shoulders, he stepped back, taking his support with him.

Angelle sank against the beam behind her. Her legs wobbled like a newborn foal and her arms were shaking. Was she supposed to dance like this?

She drew a badly needed breath, leaning her head against the wooden frame, and a wicked grin crossed Cane's face. Oh, he knew *exactly* what he'd done. That had been his intent. The message hadn't been for Brady—it had been for *her*.

"We'll pick this up later," he promised, and just like that, she was more than ready for round two.

Bring it on, city boy.

• • •

After kissing Angelle senseless, Cane watched Brady tug her

onto the dance floor. Jealousy pitched and roiled in his gut, but he didn't look away. He didn't have to. Despite the ease with which the former lovers fell into each other's arms, Cane knew whose bed she'd be in tonight.

His.

Anticipation had him antsy, eager to drag her away before she changed her mind. But he wouldn't rush this. He'd give Brady this moment. After all, it had to be hell losing a woman like Angelle. And Cane was man enough to share her attention for a few minutes. Especially since she wasn't really even his.

So it didn't matter that they looked good together, spinning and laughing as their hands formed little windows to stare into each other's eyes. The way their feet pistoned up and down in sync, hinting at a shared history, didn't rankle. And when the other couples widened the circle, clapping for the reunion of Cane's woman and her ex, it didn't even faze him.

It certainly didn't have him wanting to punch a hole through the post behind his head.

Envy, jealousy, and possession were foreign emotions to him. They were for henpecked men in relationships. They didn't suit him, and Cane didn't like them one bit. Women generally came easy for Cane, but Angelle had made him work. That was all this was. Soon, those unwanted feelings would be a thing of the past.

The all-consuming intensity with which he wanted Angelle would be gone, too. This unmatched craving was merely the result of long months imagining what it would be like with his favorite redhead. But after he spent a night holding her in his arms, and once he heard her scream his name, and saw that beautiful, sated look cross her angelic face, the need to have her, to own her, would fade.

It had to.

Things would go back to normal. In three days, they'd drive home to Magnolia Springs as friends. Friends who happened to have shared a crazy week and a hell of a night between the sheets. Guilt pricked his conscience, but he ignored it. Angelle knew the score. She may have a crush, but there was no way a woman like her could want *forever* with a man like him anyway. When this was over, she'd return to her normal life as a firefighter, only now with her family off her back, and the hottest damn memory she could imagine. Who knows, maybe their hoax would even push her to start dating again.

Cane didn't want to analyze why that thought made him see red, so instead he focused on the life *he* would go back to. Days filled with easy women, no commitments, no attachments, and no emotion.

He *really* didn't want to analyze why that life suddenly felt so empty.

Chapter Thirteen

The barn had always been Angelle's sanctuary. A quiet place to go and think, to get away from the world, especially after Amber died. Back when her family raised horses, her best friend had lived in one of the stalls. She'd feed Diamond carrots and confess her darkest secrets, and he'd agree with his dark, soulful eyes that the world did indeed suck sometimes. Later in high school and into college, when her parents grew older and it became more of a storage shed, the barn had still been her safe place. Many nights Angie would sneak away to sleep up in the loft, surrounded by memories and the sweet smell of hay and aged wood.

It was during those nights that she planned her first time. The entire thing, laid out.

The lighting (scented candles, naturally), the bedding (the soft comforter from her bed), and the soundtrack. Oh yes, a soundtrack was needed. It was the most crucial aspect. She'd seen enough romance movies to know the right song set the mood. It became a strange hobby of sorts through the years, fiddling with different songs, selecting only the best ones. A

little "U Got It Bad" by Usher, "How Do I Live" by LeAnn
Rimes, even "I'll Make Love to You" by Boys II Men, and
"Let's Get It On" by Barry White.

All slow and seductive…and completely wrong now.

None of those songs fit Cane or the slightly manic feelings
he triggered inside her. He was more like "Wild Thing" by
Tone-Loc, making her a whole lot of "Firework" by Katy Perry.
Right now, Angie felt as if her colors—along with everything
else—*were* about to burst. Like a live wire was sitting just
under her skin, buzzing and humming. Electric. But a plan
was a plan, and a girl didn't wait twenty-six *freaking* years
for something to happen only to get sidetracked at the very
last second. Tonight would be absolutely perfect. Just like her
fantasy.

"Um, I have a few things I want to do first," she said as
Cane flicked off the engine. They'd ridden home from the
festival in tense silence, but unlike on the drive from Magnolia
Springs, this had been the *good* kind of tension. The kind that
made Angelle's tummy tight with anticipation, anxiety, and
excitement. "Do you mind waiting out here?"

With only the faint glow from the streetlight, Cane's face
was in shadows. She couldn't see his expression, but his voice,
low and raspy, had her wanting to strip naked right there.
"Darlin', I've waited five months for this night. I think I can
handle a few more minutes."

A strangled sound, half-breath and half-whimper, passed
from her lips. This man was dangerous. She'd always known
that. But for once, Angie was feeling a little reckless herself.

"I-I'll be right back," she said, tossing her seat belt aside
and throwing open the passenger door. She didn't need to see
Cane's face to know he was grinning.

The moment her feet touched the ground, she was
running. She only slowed inside so she didn't terrify her
parents. Luckily, their hearing wasn't quite what it used to

be, and by speed walking on tiptoe, she was able to dash down the hall and into her room without sounding an alarm. Leaning her head against the closed bedroom door, Angelle released a shaky breath and declared, "Holy crap, I'm about to have sex."

She blinked once, twice, three times. Then, with a wide smile stretched across her face, she pushed off the door.

Grabbing a huge duffel bag from inside her closet, she ran around tossing items inside. "Flashlight, sex CD, fuzzy socks in case it gets cold…" Folding her rather large comforter proved to be a bit of a challenge, but it was part of the fantasy. Plus, she really didn't want to lie on dirt or splintered wood. Splinters in the butt did *not* say sexy to her.

Under the sink in her bathroom was a treasure trove of scented candles. Grabbing the four nearest, she shoved them inside along with a lighter, then scurried back to her room. All she was missing was protection and wardrobe. Thanks to her embarrassing, *fabulous* roommate, she had both. Sliding open the drawer, Angelle dug out the string of silver packets from where she'd buried them days ago, so sure she'd never have a use for them. A laugh bubbled in her throat as she added them to her bag, then she turned back and stared at her costume options.

Green lace, black leather, purple silk. Without a doubt, the black leather screamed Cane Robicheaux. The problem was it *didn't* scream Angelle. She'd feel like an imposter. One that could likely end up chafed in an uncomfortable spot. *Nix the leather.*

It was a tough call between the remaining two. While she loved purple, and the feel of silk was divine, Sherry had said green was Angelle's color. It matched her eyes, set off her hair, and the lace felt naughty against her fingertips. That could work.

Stripping out of her jeans and blouse, Angie contorted,

wiggled, and adjusted herself into the lingerie. Prior to this, the sexiest thing she'd ever worn was a Victoria's Secret nightgown. Lacey had bought her the nightie when she graduated—and it'd had considerably more fabric.

Daring a glance into the mirror, her eyes widened. She may as well be naked! Granted, that was the designer's point, but staring at her reflection it suddenly became very real what she was about to do. And who she was about to stand in front of in this uber-revealing getup.

Shaking her hands, Angelle blew out a breath. She cracked her neck and nodded at the mirror. "I can do this," she told herself. "I'm fearless." She turned to the side, glimpsed her exposed backside, and winced. "I'm one sexy, redheaded bitch."

Angie rolled her eyes at how *un*sexy she sounded. The girls Cane usually slept with probably didn't require pep talks in the mirror before getting it on. Picking up her hairbrush, she fluffed and teased her hair. A dab of cherry lip gloss, a pinch of the cheeks, one squirt of perfume, and a silk robe later, she was ready. Or as ready as she would ever be.

Footsteps bouncy with anxiety and anticipation, she made it back down the hall as quietly as when she'd entered. She carefully pried opened the front door. Cane was just where she'd left him, sitting in his truck, the engine off. His head was leaned back against the seat, and she briefly wondered if he'd fallen asleep. That would be a definite mood killer. But at the *click* of the front door closing, he bolted straight up.

It was cold. Angelle was wearing a skimpy, silk robe and lace underneath. But she was sweating. She wished that in her rush to begin the sexy times that she would've remembered the porch light. Shadows still filled the cab and clung to his face, hiding any hint of his expression.

Was his gaze appreciative, or disappointed?

Had she taken too long to get ready? Had she totally

misread the situation?

Could he have possibly changed his mind?

Cane was a man—an extremely sexual man—so Angie doubted it. But then, this was happening to *her*, and Murphy's Law defined her life, so anything was possible. Thankfully, before she could drive herself completely insane with questions, Cane's door opened. Soon his long-legged stride carried him over the drive to where she stood, practically shaking, on the top step of the porch. His gaze traveled over every inch of her frame, from the top of her head, to her red-painted toenails, and then back up.

"You're the most beautiful woman I've ever seen."

Nerves had her smirking, brushing the compliment aside. But Cane shook his head and brought his finger to the side of her face. Slowly, he glided it over the swell of her cheek and down the sensitive skin of her throat. "Most. Beautiful."

Angelle forgot all about the chill in the air, thanks to the heat in his eyes. He wanted this to happen as badly as she did. He wanted *her*.

"I'm not a saint," he told her, cupping his hand around her neck. His thumb lightly teased the indent where her pulse fluttered. "I've been with a lot of women. But *none* of them has ever gotten to me the way you have. You're under my skin, angel."

His words made her shiver, and Cane shrugged out of his leather jacket. Almost reverent eyes glued to hers, he placed the jacket warmed by his body heat around her shoulders, enveloping Angelle with her favorite scent. The small, chivalrous gesture spoke volumes as to the kind of lover he would be, and it gave her the courage to say, "Follow me to the barn."

Cane raised a dark eyebrow. Angelle felt a naughty smile twist her lips, daring him to argue. With a matching grin, he took her duffel bag, and then her hand, and fell into step beside her. "I'll follow you anywhere, hellcat."

Harsh gravel gave way to soft grass as they crept around the side of the house. Under her bare feet, the soft, damp earth tickled. The air she drew into her lungs crackled with awareness. Being with Cane was a sensory explosion—and the night hadn't even begun.

Imagining what *sex* with him would be like gave her true palpitations. Fainting was suddenly a real possibility.

Dear God, please don't let me faint.

Dappled moonlight reflected off the old barn and once they reached it, Cane stopped outside the entrance. "What now, angel?"

She glanced at the site for her seduction plans and sank her teeth into her lip. She still needed to set things up. With a wince she replied, "Mind waiting a few more minutes?"

His eyes crinkled as he chuckled. This was *so* not going as she'd planned.

Part of her considered abandoning her fantasy altogether, but Angie knew she'd regret it. There could be no do-overs, no second chances. You only lose your virginity once. And tonight, she wanted no regrets. "It's just…I want everything to be perfect. For us. I kind of have a *thing* prepared…that's why I brought the bag." She fiddled with the belt on her robe and added, "It'll only take a second, I promise."

Cane grinned and slid the bag off his massive shoulder. "A thing, huh? Gotta tell you, I never took you for the kinky type." Angelle's face flamed as he handed the bag back, and he placed a knuckle under her chin. Gaze soft but serious he said, "I was teasing you, darlin'. Whatever you need to make tonight the best you've ever had, I'm down for it."

The best I've ever had. That should be easy to accomplish.

A pang of worry hit at the thought, but she brushed it aside, quickly leaning up and kissing his cheek. "It won't take long." Then, before she lost her nerve—or revealed her secret too soon—she bolted inside.

Tugging out the flashlight she'd packed, Angelle clicked it on and easily made her way toward the ladder Ryan had built. As she carefully navigated over the broken step, lugging her bag of essentials to the loft, an annoying voice preached inside her head.

You need to tell him you're a virgin, it hissed. *And sooner rather than later.*

"I will tell him," she hissed back, throwing her bag over the top rail. "Just…not yet. This is huge. On the off-chance Cane decides it's *too* huge and calls it off, I at least want to get a hint of the good stuff. Maybe even round a few bases. *Then* I'll tell him."

She waited a moment, but no further scolding came. Shoulders back, she set to work.

Angie spread the comforter over a pile of hay and dust, then placed candles at strategic spots around the loft, maximizing mood yet avoiding the unsexy risk of burn. After lighting the wicks, she grabbed the ancient boom box she'd kept up there since she was eleven and plugged it in. The final touch was sliding in her sex CD.

It was old school—no iPods for her—but then *she* was kind of old school, too.

Looking around the softly lit loft, she realized her fantasy had come to life. Everything was exactly how she'd pictured it. And the mystery man from her vision finally had a face. One that was handsome as hell. With the room arranged and no further reason to stall, Angelle cleared her throat. "I'm ready!"

Heavy footsteps immediately drew near. Angelle quickly slipped off Cane's leather jacket, followed by her silk robe, then directed the flashlight's beam toward the ladder. "Up here," she called, glancing around again in a sudden panic.

Should she pose?

Lie down on the comforter, or stand with her hip jutted and boobs thrust out?

Why hadn't she asked Sherry more questions?

Spinning in a circle, she surveyed her options and decided to go with the makeshift bed. Beds screamed passion, right? Hitting play on the stereo, Angie collapsed to the floor and squirmed to find the perfect seductive pose that said, *Come and get me.*

Cane's footsteps reached the ladder as the intro to "Crash Into Me" by Dave Matthews Band began. A noise that sounded suspiciously like a chuckle came from below. But then, all she cared about was that it *came from just below.*

"Watch the broken third step," she advised, her voice pitched much higher than normal, as heat flashed over her skin. Each creak that followed meant he was getting closer, until finally, his head peeked above the stairs.

He grinned. "Did you make a sex mixed tape?"

"Maybe." Cane's grin widened as he took the last step, pulling himself up onto the loft, and she admitted, "Okay, yes, I did. I made a sex tape."

When a full smile broke across his face, Angie realized how that had sounded. "*No!* I mean a mixed tape. A *music* tape. I made a musical mixed tape for sex."

Awkward Angie for the win.

She blew out a breath, wishing that for just once in her life she could do something important and not make a fool of herself. Lifting her hands to encompass the room, she said, "This is the thing." Angelle shrugged a shoulder as she dropped her arms to fiddle with her see-through outfit. "You're kind of fulfilling a fantasy for me."

Cane glanced around, but his gaze quickly returned. Hot eyes traced the lines of her body and the thick knot in his throat bobbed as he swallowed. "Angel, it's *you* who are fulfilling mine."

Boom. Any doubts that may've lingered were blown straight to hell. Stark honesty shone on his face and sincerity rang in his voice. This was right. It *felt* right. Finally, the trifecta she'd been waiting for—passion, excitement, and that gut-level truth—was all in one package. And what made it even better (though she'd never admit it aloud, at least not yet) was that Angie realized she'd fallen head over boots in love with him.

Feeling more confident, more daring than she ever had before, Angelle skimmed her nail over the lace edge of her bodice. Cane's eyes hungrily followed the movement, and she grinned. "Then what are you waiting for?"

• • •

Holy hell. He'd unleashed a vixen. A fiery, flirtatious, sexy as shit, vixen. And damn, did she take his breath away. Stepping out of his boots, Cane left them near the ladder as he slowly made his way to the bed his angel had set out.

Candlelight, corny music, sex in a hayloft…he would've thought he'd entered a poorly scripted Skinemax movie had it not been for the woman on the blanket. This scene fit Angelle. And while slow and sweet wasn't what he'd had in mind, he'd be glad to make her fantasy come true. Especially since it implied no one else had.

Sinking to his knees beside her, Cane ran his hand over the creamy skin of her thigh. "This is your night, angel. Tell me what you want."

Desire sparked in those haunting green eyes. Pushing to a kneeling position she said, "You, Cane. Just you." Then, fisting the cotton of his shirt in her hands, she yanked him forward.

Angelle's hot mouth slammed into his. Her hands seemed to be everywhere at once. Tugging at his shirt. Fumbling with his belt. Pulling him closer. She attacked with an almost crazed intensity. Aggressive. Wild. The hellcat had most definitely come out to play.

And Cane loved it.

He slid his tongue along the column of her throat. A voice in his head warned to dial it back. To slow things down. But he told that voice to go to hell. Angie's whimpers and moans were much better guides.

"Right here," he told her, knotting his fingers in her hair so he could look in her eyes. "*This* is my fantasy. Breathing you in, holding you in my arms. Hearing you moan my name." Another moan escaped, and he grinned. Ducking his head, he whispered against her ear, "And it's about to get a whole lot better."

Pushing to his feet, he reached back and yanked his shirt over his head. As Cane made quick work of his jeans, his skin prickled from the hunger in Angelle's focused gazed. He tossed his clothes in a pile near his shoes and turned back, eager to pick up where they'd left off.

Angelle's eyes widened.

Cane paused, watching as she licked her lips. Her gaze dipped to his black boxer briefs and bounced away. As he walked back, a nudge that something was off messed with his head. But he ignored it. Sinking down beside her, he slid her hair to one shoulder and pressed a kiss against her skin. She shivered. "Everything okay?"

"Mmm hmm." Angelle nodded and her lips made a smacking sound. "Perfect."

Chalking the weird vibe up to nerves, he tugged the thin straps of her lingerie off her shoulders. Goose bumps trailed his kisses down her arm and over her collarbone. Every inch of Angelle was soft. And she smelled so damn good. Reaching around her back, Cane flicked the clasp on her top.

She gasped and stiffened in his arms.

This time, an alarm rang inside his head.

"Hey, we'll go slow." He drew lazy circles over the soft skin of her shoulders, wanting to assure her. Had he moved too fast? He didn't think so, but he sure as hell wasn't going to mess this up now. "We've got all night."

Angelle shook her head and then smiled. "No, it's good. I'm good."

Her eyes held a different story. Slowing things down, wanting the vixen back, Cane sought her mouth. He kissed her long and deep, and as he'd hoped, she melted in his arms. He waited until she became restless, squirming and seeking more. Then, while his tongue teased hers, Cane pulled the lace down.

Hands aching to move, to touch, Cane clenched the fabric, waiting for resistance. Instead, Angie squirmed again. He grinned against her mouth and whispered, "There's my hellcat."

She wiggled closer, leaning her body nearer his hand, and Cane was happy to oblige. Brushing his knuckles against the swell of her breasts, he teased her, knowing what she wanted. And when she moaned a plea into his mouth, he finally cupped them in his hands. Lowering his head, he licked a wet line in the valley between them, and as she shuddered and writhed, her head fell back as she exclaimed, "Oh, God."

That damn alarm in his head got louder.

Cane wanted her responsive. He wanted her to enjoy his touch. But something felt…off.

Leaning back, he stared into her dazed eyes. Angelle's cheeks were flushed, her lips red from his kisses, and when her gaze flicked to his briefs, he saw wonder cross her face.

"Angel?"

That was all he said, but she froze. Looking away, she closed her eyes, seeming to understand his unspoken question. Time stopped. What he was thinking couldn't be possible. There had to be another explanation. But when her eyes opened, and she turned back with a face full of fear and hope, the warning bell rang so loud it nearly drowned out the words, "I'm a virgin."

She didn't say anything else. Neither did he. Her sex soundtrack switched over to Maroon 5's "She Will Be Loved," but other than the song, the barn was silent. Angelle watched him, eyes growing rounder, teeth sinking so far into that bottom lip he feared she'd draw blood. But all he could do was kneel there. In shock.

This was way deeper than Cane ever intended. He'd never been anyone's first before, but he knew what it meant. What it would do. This wouldn't just be a fun night or a sexy fantasy. This would bond them emotionally, more than they already were. It would let her in on an intimate level, a soul-deep level, which was much more than he'd bargained for.

Besides that, taking Angelle's virginity would be a dick move. There was no other way to look at it. Later he'd try to figure out how in the hell she could possibly still be a virgin, but right now, all he knew was that only an asshole would take something she'd obviously been saving. As much as he wanted this to happen—and *damn*, did he want it to—it wouldn't be right. Doing so would almost guarantee her pain. And that went against every vow and promise he'd made to himself as a man.

"I think—"

"No, Cane. Whatever you're about to say, hear me out first, okay?" Placing her palm on his cheek, she forced him to look at her. "I know what I'm doing. I'm not drunk or misguided. I'm not breakable, or a saint, or untouchable, either. This isn't a religious thing or some random pledge I took. It just never felt right." A look of determination crossed her face and she leaned in to kiss him, hard. Pulling back she said, "Now it does. I *want* you to be my first. Please…make love to me?"

Shit. How in the hell could he say no to that? Especially

when every part of him wanted the same damn thing.

This was a fork in the road. There'd be no going back from this decision. But he could no more deny her than he could deny himself.

Ignoring the voice screaming in his head, muting the ringing alarm, and flipping off the caveman thrill of knowing he'd be her first, Cane cupped her shoulders. "I'll make it good for you. I promise."

A beautiful, knowing smile broke across her face as she said, "I'm counting on it."

. . .

Only one of Angelle's candles remained lit. All the others had burned out. They'd exhausted every song on her sex soundtrack—*twice*—and then passed out. Thankfully without setting the barn on fire. Stretching his neck, Cane looked down at the woman asleep in his arms, a sated smile still curving her swollen mouth. He ducked his head and kissed it.

A happy sigh of contentment escaped her parted lips as she curled into his side. Cane waited a moment to see if she was awake, then, convinced she was down for the count, grabbed the edge of the blanket and threw it over their bodies. He stared at the support beams overhead and inwardly cursed.

He'd screwed up.

He'd taken her virginity. He'd sensed she felt more for him than she should, but he'd done it anyway. This hadn't been a casual hookup for Angelle. She would never forget tonight—and now, neither would he.

Guilt and protectiveness warred with a mounting sense of dread. It was true he hadn't forced her into anything. And he'd made no promises for the future. So really, tonight should be no different from any other night he'd spent with a willing woman. And Angelle *had* been willing. He'd been ready to walk, and she'd convinced him to stay.

None of that made him feel any less like an ass.

Angelle's weight sank more into him and her lips made a soft smacking noise. Her breaths were slow and even. Clearly, she wasn't wasting time overthinking things. She wasn't lying there, asking for forever. Maybe this was all him. Once he got his head straight, maybe everything would be fine. They'd finish up the ruse as planned, then leave in a few days as friends. Good friends who happened to know each other really well.

Cane's guilt lessened a fraction, and he pressed his lips against her hair.

Her drowsy head shifted. "Is it morning?" she asked, kissing the tattoo over his chest. A spot she'd shown a lot of special attention.

Chuckling, Cane tucked the blanket tightly around her gorgeous body. From the dim glow on the wood, he'd say it was just around dawn. "Go back to sleep. You have a long day ahead of you." He smirked at the ceiling. "And you had a very adventurous night."

Angelle laughed softly and pinched the skin along his rib cage. "Okay," she said, snuggling against him. "But only for another hour or so." She threw her leg over his hip, yawned long and loud, then, wrapping an arm around his waist, whispered, "Love you."

Cane's body turned to stone as Angelle's soft snores filled the loft.

Chapter Fourteen

The main road leading out of Bon Terre had been foggy and empty. The interstate headed toward New Orleans wasn't much different. Cane was driving home, jaw flexed, self-hate roiling in his gut, and only a smattering of cars had passed him on the highway. Everyone else was still in bed. Warm and sleeping, maybe making love. Wrapped around the person they cared about—like Cane should have been. Instead, he was alone in his truck, with nothing but disgust and shame to keep him company.

If he hadn't been an asshole before, he sure as hell was one now.

Angelle Prejean loved him. Never could he have imagined a woman saying those words to him, much less a woman like her. She was the type of woman who could star in those sappy movies his sisters loved. Good, kind, adorable. Sexy as hell. And she deserved a man from those movies, the kind who could give her a Hollywood ending. The only thing Cane could offer was a good roll in the hay. But even though he'd known that all along, he'd still pursued her.

Angelle also deserved for her first time to have been with

someone who would say those three words back. Who *could* say those three words back. Not an asshole who'd leave the moment the deed was done, treating her like she was a damn booty call.

Cane cursed under his breath.

Some cold-blooded shit. That's what it was. She'd given him her virginity, and he'd taken off like a bat out of hell. Or like the asshole he'd proven himself to be.

The kicker was he didn't even know *why* he'd left. It had been basic instinct. Angelle had whispered her sleep confession, passed out again, and then he'd bolted. No note, no explanation. Just took off, knowing the whole time he pulled on his clothes, slid on his shoes, and nearly busted his ass on the missing step of the ladder, that it was wrong. But he'd done it anyway. And now, it was too late. He'd been driving for almost two hours. He couldn't undo his actions.

His right hand closed around the cell phone sitting in his lap. It hadn't rung once. Surely she was awake by now, had realized he'd left. But she hadn't called. He could do the honorable thing and call *her,* but what the hell would he say? Raking a hand through his hair, Cane thought about his next step. No way was he coming back from this. Maybe, eventually, Angelle would forgive him enough to tolerate his presence, but that friendship he'd wanted? That real, honest relationship he'd never had with a woman but had come to believe was something he *needed* in his life, at least when that woman was Angelle? That got blown to shit the second he walked out of the barn.

His mind fired up the image burned into his retinas that hours of driving hadn't shook. When he'd first put his feet on the rung to leave, he'd hesitated for a brief second. In the glow of the flashlight, Angelle's hair had shone like a fiery halo, and a soft smile had curved her mouth. An electrical jolt had hit his chest at just how perfect she was. Then she'd made a noise and shifted—and he'd fled.

Spying the sign declaring Magnolia Springs only thirty-five miles away, he slammed his hand against the steering wheel. "Fuck!"

What in the hell was he doing?

He was leaving her to pick up the pieces, alone. Heartbroken and confused. He was letting down the entire town, not to mention all the kids hoping to see Papa Noel. And he was disrespecting the family who'd taken him in, against their better judgment, and who had reminded him of all the things he'd been missing.

Noting the upcoming exit, Cane flicked the turn signal and gunned the engine. It looked like he was becoming well acquainted with the interstate today.

He shook his head as he glanced at the clock. By the time he got back to Bon Terre, Angelle would be at the parade ground. The entire town would be there, too, believing God only knew what about him and their so-called engagement. But Cane didn't care. He'd walk straight into the firing squad, knowing it was going to be awkward as hell, because that's what a man did. The kind of man he wanted to be, and the kind of man he'd vowed to be.

He would find Angelle and explain. Apologize for his actions and for leading her on, and then pray she forgave him for hurting her. He'd get her to understand why he left even when *he* couldn't.

And if she tells you to go to hell?

A sharp ache twisted in Cane's chest. Right underneath the yin-yang tattoo Angelle loved so much.

If she refused to forgive him, then he'd have to accept it. But he wouldn't let her down. He'd agreed to come on this trip and help her win over her hometown, and as long as his mother's ring was on her finger, Cane was still her fake fiancé.

For better or worse, right?

Chapter Fifteen

Delightfully sore muscles fought back as Angelle languidly stretched from her cozy pallet on the floor. Early morning light filtered through slats of aged wood, casting the loft in a soft, romantic glow. Or maybe that was just Angie's love-addled brain. Joy bubbled in her chest as she thought about last night. It had been nothing short of perfection.

Sighing happily, she surveyed the remains of her night of seduction. Candles long burned out, Sherry's lingerie torn and abandoned in the corner—it appeared she owed her roommate one new nightie—and her rumpled, familiar comforter, now smelling of Cane's cologne. Bunching a section in her hands, she sniffed with a grin. The only thing missing from the best night of her life was the man himself. Her yummy fiancé.

Of course, he was her *fake* fiancé, but somehow in light of the night they'd shared, that detail didn't seem as significant as it had a few days ago. She hadn't woken up crazy, or certifiable like his ex Becca—wedding bells weren't ringing in her ears, and bridesmaid dresses weren't flashing before her eyes. But she *was* in love with him. That truth became easier to admit the more she thought it, so assuming he was out answering nature's call, she whispered it aloud.

"I'm in love with Cane Robicheaux."

Now she needed to find the right time to tell *him*. See if his feelings were anywhere close to hers. She knew it was a long shot, but when they'd made love, Cane had stroked her with an almost worshipful intensity. Not an inch of her skin had been untouched by his lips, tongue, or fingertips. Even when it had gotten wild—warmth flooded her skin as she remembered a few rowdy moments in particular—he'd stared at her as if he really saw her. Genuinely cared about her.

Her grin widened as she pushed to her feet, only to have it drop a shade when she looked around again. Her faux-betrothed's pit stop was taking longer than she would've expected. "Cane?"

When he didn't answer and she didn't hear rustling outside the barn, Angelle decided he must be in the main house fixing breakfast. The man was a phenomenal cook…and today *was* a special day, after all. For the last eighteen years, it had been edged with sadness, but maybe this was just another sign that she'd somehow turned a corner.

Her empty stomach rumbled as she pondered when Sherry might have slipped him intel about today. She'd planned to tell him yesterday before matters that were much more urgent presented themselves. Angelle grinned. Stretching again, muscles she hadn't known existed fussed in protest, but her smile grew with every twinge of discomfort. It had been worth it. So very, *very* worth it.

"Maybe we can squeeze in round two before we leave," she said, slipping on her robe. Knotting the belt, she corrected herself. "Or more like round five."

With a happy bounce in her step, she set to work cleaning up because having her parents stumble upon their love nest was *not* an option. It was true she was an adult, but there were just some topics that should never be discussed with one's mother. Or one's father. *Ever.*

   Grabbing the duffel bag, Angie began filling it with mementos. She stupidly wanted to save it all. Her first time had turned out better than she could've imagined, and while the props hadn't been what made it so—that was all Cane— they'd borne witness to the moment her life had shifted. This was the start of something new. The warmth swimming in her chest and gushing through her veins was proof of that.

   As it turned out, taking a chance on Cane had been the best gamble of her life.

   Sending Amber a silent thank-you, she placed the last candle in her bag.

   Sherry's torn lingerie and the empty silver packets were balled for the trash. The comforter refolded and shoved inside the bag. A prickle of worry formed when Cane still hadn't returned from the kitchen, but Angelle sent it packing with a shake of her head. Maybe he'd run into her parents and gotten sidetracked, though she really hoped not. He must've taken his clothes because they were gone, which meant he wasn't walking around half-naked, but unfortunately, she couldn't say the same.

   Mental note: add *change of clothes* to future sex to-do lists.

   Luckily, Angie's parents woke with the sun and usually left early during the festival. Figuring she was in the clear, she shouldered the massive duffel bag and took off for the main house. When she opened the back door, the scent of bacon and fresh baked bread hit her nose. Her knees went weak.

   "There you are. I—" The sight of her parents made Angelle freeze in the doorway. Cool air blew up the hem of her robe, making it *pointedly* obvious the thin garment was all she was wearing. "Mama, Daddy. I'd assumed you'd be at the park by now."

Stepping fully inside, she tugged the door closed behind her and folded an arm across her chest, praying her face wasn't as crimson as she imagined it was. A glance at the microwave clock said it was six thirty-five. Earlier than she'd thought.

Mama set her coffee mug on the counter and cleared her throat. "We're heading out as soon as your daddy finishes his second cup." She gestured toward her husband, who nodded, making a point not to stare too long in Angie's direction. Every tangle in her hair and each abrasion on her fair skin from Cane's stubble felt magnified. A knowing smile flirted at her mama's mouth. "And where'd your fiancé get off to so early this morning? I see his truck's gone."

Embarrassment faded as Angelle's eyebrows snapped together. "What?"

She turned to look out the kitchen window, her lips parted in confusion. Mama was right. Cane's truck was gone.

What the heck? She narrowed her eyes on the empty spot in the driveway where Cane's truck once sat as if it would miraculously give her an answer. Because there had to be one. A reason why he'd left that made sense. *Any* explanation other than the one she was thinking. The one that made her stomach sink to her toes. But what?

He had to have left early. Mama asking meant neither of her parents had seen him, and they'd been awake for at least an hour. It was possible he was just up the road shopping, getting…getting…getting *what?*

There was nothing he could need this early in the morning. Everything he could possibly want for breakfast was already in the house. The chickens in the backyard provided a steady supply of eggs, and her mama kept all the staples. Even if she hadn't, every store in Bon Terre was a ten-to-fifteen-minute round trip. Tops.

Could he have driven back to Magnolia Springs? Angelle's

chest tightened at the thought of a possible emergency with his sisters, or even their family restaurant. But then, why wouldn't he have woken her up? She'd grown to think of his family as her adopted second one, and as a citizen of Magnolia Springs, Robicheaux's was important to her.

Angie's vision swam as the room tilted. There'd been no note. She'd cleaned the entire loft, so she would've found it. Fear lodged in her throat.

This wasn't happening.

Dazed, and 100 percent in denial that the man she loved, the man she'd been so sure felt the same, had ditched her, Angie turned back to her parents. She caught them exchanging a look. *No*. The last thing she needed was them sounding the alarm and rounding up the posse. She needed to think, to process—and she needed to do that *alone*.

"Oh, that's right." Forcing a laugh that sounded off even to her ears, she took a shaky step toward the hall, squeezing her bag against her chest as if it could somehow shield her from pain. "Cane wanted to watch the sunrise over Bayou Teche."

The excuse was weak. She knew it, and she could tell her parents knew it. But it wasn't as weak as her next words. "He'll be back."

A sob built in her core as she took another step.

He'll be back.

She could feel the pressure mounting, rising with each foot of ground she gained. When she reached the doorway, it came out as a strangled moan and Angelle clamped her lips into a wavering smile. Her daddy's jaw ticked as he set down the newspaper. Pity lined both their faces. She shook her head. "He'll be back."

She bolted down the hall.

He'll be back.

The words kept repeating as hot tears blinded her path.

Flinging open the door, she closed and locked it behind her, the words becoming a mantra as tremors rocked her body. Angie's legs gave out. The mantra became a prayer as she sank to the floor, drew up her knees, and curled herself into a ball, fighting for breath.

He'll be back.

But even as she thought it, wished it, *prayed* it, she knew the truth. Cane had left her. And she was an idiot. A brokenhearted idiot who'd fallen for the playboy. Oh, he was good; she gave him that. Cane had never promised her a thing. That had all been Angie. She'd just assumed.

Even now, faced with the truth, her mind refused to accept it. Had he really spent a week with her family just to get in her pants? She didn't know if she should be shocked, flattered, or appalled that she warranted such behavior. But more than anything, more than the humiliation of knowing she'd fallen for the lie, for the game, and that her own parents had witnessed it, what hurt her the most was that she'd honestly thought they'd become friends. She'd certainly grown to consider Cane as such—but friends didn't do this. They didn't act as though they gave a shit, and then take it all away. They didn't leave without a word.

Didn't she at least warrant a note? A phone call? Some kind of explanation?

As if on cue, her cell phone buzzed on the dresser. She'd left it there in her mad rush of preparation last night. She knew she should reach up and get it. Read whatever lie he'd concocted to explain his actions. She'd *just* told herself she wanted to know. But did she really?

The phone buzzed again.

Placing her hands on the ground, Angelle decided it was time to put on her big girl panties. If she was mature enough to handle sleeping with the man, she should be mature enough to deal with the fallout. Maybe it wouldn't be as bad as she feared. And then if it was, well, better she know now. Rip off the Band-Aid.

As she clamored to her feet, she glimpsed her reflection in the mirror. Whisker burn and swollen lips collided with red-rimmed puffy eyes and ghostly pale skin. She looked like an unhinged extra on *The Walking Dead*. Grabbing the phone without reading the message, her eyes fell on the bottle cap from the night she babysat Sadie with Cane. Without thinking, she picked it up and closed her hand around it. The phone buzzed again.

Hoping the talisman would bring her luck, she inhaled a deep breath of courage and glanced down. A series of messages waited. Scrolling through them, she searched for the name of the man she loved. The closest she came was his baby sister. Tapping on Sherry's text, Angelle's eyes pooled with fresh tears.

Her best friend and roommate's face filled the screen, blowing a kiss over the words, "HAPPY BIRTHDAY, FUTURE SISTER-IN-LAW! XOXO."

$$\bullet \bullet \bullet$$

People of every age and size packed Les Acadiens Park. It was day two of the Cracklin Festival and while tourists strolled, children screamed, and a crew of Bon Terre's finest manned booths, the rest of the town stood near the large stage at the back of the field. Although the mayor was at the microphone, going over activities to be done that day and during tomorrow's parade and Fais Do Do, Cane knew the focus of the crowd was directed at him.

Or, more like split equally between him and Angelle, who was not standing beside him. And who was standing *way* too close to her ex.

Cane wanted to punch something. Neither of them had

spotted him yet, even with the whispers of the crowd. He was behind them, several feet to the left, far enough not to make a scene but close enough to watch Brady's arm flirt with holding her. By his watch, the man had moved to put it around Angelle's waist three times. If he ever finally did, Cane wouldn't be responsible for his actions.

Hands fisted in his pockets, tension knotted in his shoulders, Cane knew he deserved this. The jealous fire raging in his blood. The torment of knowing he'd caused Angelle pain and watching another man try to pick up the pieces. This was his payback. Seeing Angelle's haunted profile, her smile broken. *He'd* done that to her. He really was an ass.

A dumb ass, too, because he'd actually thought the desperate need he'd had, the consuming possession he'd felt, would disappear once he'd had her. It hadn't. Hours spent staring at the cold, open highway proved how flawed that logic had been. One night with Angelle hadn't gotten her out of his system. If anything, she'd only burrowed deeper.

Right now, the need to hold her in his arms, to kiss away that pain was so strong Cane nearly shook with it. But he'd bide his time. He'd wait for her dad to finish and the group to disband, and then he'd speak with her. Alone. Without her adoring ex clinging to her like a leech.

As if the slime could hear his thoughts, Brady lifted his head. He scanned the crowd and when his eyes locked on Cane, an emotion akin to hate sparked in the *good* doctor's eyes.

Maybe the man wasn't the pushover Cane had pegged him to be. Behind him, Ryan and Troy stood a concerned guard, also clearly in the know that something had gone down. Only the fact that Cane was still standing with two functional testicles proved she hadn't confessed the *whole* story.

Brady narrowed his eyes, a clear warning for him to stay away, then turned back to the stage. A mild case of respect formed for the man…but not enough for Cane to heed the warning. This wasn't any of Brady's damn business. And the fact that he wanted to be Angelle's soft place to land had Cane entertaining thoughts of running his head into the damn stage.

"I guess that's about it," Angelle's father said, snapping Cane's focus back to the front. "Anyone needing a costume for tomorrow's parade please see Dottie at the information desk. Other than that, y'all go on and have fun!"

With a cheer, the crowd dispersed, breaking into groups to chat. Cane strode forward.

Thoughts jumbled as he wove a path to where she stood. He'd trying calling from the road, but she never answered. Straight to voice mail. Now the long speech he'd prepared sounded pathetic in his ears. None of it mattered, other than he was sorry. So damn sorry.

A foot away from reaching Angelle, Troy stepped in front of him. "Maybe this isn't the place to be doing this. I don't know what's going on—"

"You're right." Cane looked the other man in the eyes. He had sisters of his own, so he respected the gesture. But he wasn't going anywhere. "You don't."

At the sound of his voice, Angelle had stiffened. The crowd around them quieted as her head snapped in his direction. Deep green pools of hurt slayed him. They reached into his soul and begged for answers he still didn't have. The unmistakable proof of what he'd done was in those unguarded, honest eyes. Remorse lodged in Cane's throat along with his apology.

I'm sorry wasn't good enough.

This was why he'd sworn off relationships. He'd spent his entire adult life keeping good women like Angelle at a distance, the fear that he was his father's son fueling his lifestyle of no attachments. But in the end, it had all been for nothing. He'd hurt Angelle anyway.

Her eyes squeezed shut, cutting off his connection to her thoughts. Sadly, it didn't take a mind reader to know what she thought of him. She hated his guts. That truth hurt almost as much as knowing he deserved it.

Releasing a sigh, Angelle held up her hand when he moved forward. Thick lashes guarded her eyes as she said, "Not now, Cane. This festival's important to our community." A slight waver portrayed her emotions, and moistening her lips, she finished in a lowered voice, "Let's not do this now, okay?"

As much as it pained him to deny her, Cane shook his head. "No, that's not okay."

That got a reaction. Her brothers bristled as Angelle raised her eyes. Cane took a step closer, feeling like shit warmed over when she winced. She was afraid of him. They weren't just back to square one, as he'd feared—they'd flown straight off the board. But then Brady cupped her elbow in a display of protection, and Cane felt his nostrils flare.

He'd planned to do this alone, but he was man enough to grovel in front of witnesses if that's what she needed. Cane knew he'd earned every damn wall she threw up between them, and then some.

"I screwed up," he admitted loudly, taking yet another step. The crowd within hearing distance went completely silent. "I know it. You know it. The good doctor knows it, and everyone listening in right now knows it. Nothing I can do or say will change that. But we need to talk, and it has to be now. I'm not letting you go another minute, hour, or however long it'll take you to *think* you're ready to hear it, believing that any of this is your fault. It's not. This is my bullshit."

Angelle's slim shoulders shook as she brushed her hair behind her ear, gaze darting to the rapt, eavesdropping crowd. But then it returned to him, which meant *she* was listening, too. That's all Cane cared about.

He took another step, and Brady spoke up. "Look, Cane, you said your piece, but it's clear Angie doesn't want to discuss this right now. Don't you think on today of *all* days you should respect her wishes?"

Today of all days? What the hell did that mean? Confused, Cane watched the tip of Angelle's exposed ear flash red. The only possible explanation was that she *had* told her ex about last night, but if she had, that mild case of respect he'd developed for Brady vanished. If he knew what Cane had done and hadn't thrown him to the ground, pummeling his ass, then Cane's first opinion had been right. Brady wasn't a man.

Hell, Cane wanted to kick his own ass for what he'd done.

Brady shook his head in disgust. "Yeah, today. Don't you think bir—"

"Okay, we'll talk!"

Both men turned at Angelle's outburst, along with half the crowd. Eva, Lacey, and Angelle's parents walked over to join the ring of spectators, and standing straight and tall, Mr. Prejean asked, "Is there a problem here?"

"No, Daddy. Everything's fine." Angelle sent him a pointed look, one that she then turned on Brady and the rest of her family. "I'm a big girl, y'all. This is between Cane and me. Couples fight. Troy, the scraps you and Eva have gotten into are legendary. Now, the two of us are going to go talk. *Alone.* Then I expect we're all going to enjoy the festival. Okay?"

Cane couldn't deny he was impressed. A quick glance at her family proved he wasn't the only one. This wasn't the woman who'd once startled at her own shadow. Or apologized after tripping over her own two feet. The Angelle with a fisted hand on her jutted out, jean-clad hip wasn't *petite fille*, or Little Red, or Awkward Angie, the name Cane had heard whispered the last couple of days. She had a backbone and a voice and fire shooting out of her eyes. Fire she directed at him before nodding toward the edge of the field. "Come on."

Cautious optimism grew as he fell in step beside her. Angelle could've sent him packing. She could've asked one of her bodyguards to toss him on his ass. But she hadn't. She was going to hear him out.

Cane wasn't an idiot. He knew this was bad. But if she was willing to listen, maybe he could fix it. Make it right. Salvage something. He had to believe that, because after almost four hours driving round trip, he'd come to one overwhelming conclusion.

He needed Angelle. Not in a relationship, but in his life. Plain and simple.

Cane wasn't white picket fences and forever. If they were together the way she *thought* she wanted, he'd destroy her in the end. Look at what he'd already done, and that was while he was trying to protect her. But if Angelle could forgive him, if she could give him another chance, he'd be the best damn friend she'd ever had. He'd make sure no one else hurt her the way he had.

At the edge of the crowd, she turned to him. The hellcat was gone and her eyes were full of tears. His optimism went to hell. Raising her left hand, the one that held his mother's ring, she glanced at it and said, "I'm gonna make this real easy. You got what you came for, and I all but begged you for it. So let's not make a big deal out of this."

Falling tears betrayed her confident words. They rooted Cane to the ground, rendering him speechless. Any woman crying made him feel helpless, but this was *Angelle*. And she was crying because of him. That knowledge cut deeper than anything he could've imagined.

With a watery laugh, Angelle shrugged. "I should probably be thanking you, right? I mean, I got what I wanted, too. I was curious about passion, and you taught me. I couldn't have asked for a better tutor, so really, I'm lucky. I was just the idiot who forgot it was all a game." With another fake laugh, she rolled her tear-filled eyes. "Guess that's *another* thing to thank you for, then. You taught me exactly how naïve I am. So thank you, Cane. It's been an education."

Angelle's mouth tightened, her lips trying for a brave smile. The result was so far from its normal radiance it was a mockery.

Self-hate burned the back of his throat. Swallowing past the rising bile, he shook his head. "Naïve? You have the biggest heart of anyone I've ever met. You see the good in people, even when they don't have any. You're open and honest and care deeply. That's not naïve." Giving in to the fierce need to touch her, Cane stepped forward and cupped her cheek, wiping his thumb at the tears still falling. He searched her eyes, wanting to know she was listening. "Angel, that's beautiful."

Her face tightened in pain as she squeezed her eyes shut. For a brief moment, she leaned into his touch, and Cane considered pulling her into his arms like he so badly wanted to do. But then, her sad eyes opened. "Well, that beautiful heart is broken."

The words were a knife straight to *his* heart. Emotions too many to name churned in his gut, but all of them scared him shitless. And when Angelle's gaze dropped to her hand, and she began wiggling his mother's ring from her finger, true fear joined the mix.

He closed his hand around hers. "No."

She raised her eyes to his, clearly confused. "I'm letting you off the hook, Cane. Take it."

If he took back that ring, Cane knew it was over. The hoax. The fake engagement. Even the tentative friendship they'd begun to build. That ring symbolized so much more than their ruse, and every bone in his body screamed not to let her walk away until he'd made this right. But causing a scene wasn't Angelle's style. She'd rather be flayed alive than have any more of her dirty laundry aired in public. He'd caused her enough pain already; the least he could do was give her space now.

She knew he was here. He'd make sure she knew he wasn't going anywhere. He'd leave for now and regroup…

But he'd be damned if that ring left her pretty finger.

"I don't want the ring back, angel." Cane gently pushed the band over her knuckle, then grasped her fingers in his. "We don't have to do this now. I'll give you space if that's what you need. But I honor my commitments, and I gave you my word. I'm your man this week, and we're seeing this fake engagement through." He paused to let her process then added, "I also gave my word about the parade tomorrow."

Eyebrows furrowed, Angelle studied his face. "Brady already said he'd do it."

"Like hell he will," Cane spat. She flinched, and immediately he regretted his tone. It'd been automatic. Brady wasn't fooling anyone. It was clear what he wanted, but he needed to stay the hell out of Cane's business. For the next few days, that was Angelle. "*I'm* Papa Noel, and I'll be there tomorrow. You can count on that." Wanting to see her smile again, even if just for a moment, he added, "I'll be the guy in the bright red suit."

It took longer than he'd hoped, but the smallest of smiles twitched her lips. It felt like he'd won the lottery. It might not be much of a victory, but at this point, he'd take it. "You and I will talk then."

"Maybe." Angelle rocked back on the heel of her boots, her lower lip trapped between her teeth. Eyes that had once gazed at him with desire and humor now swirled with doubt and confusion. If he wanted her to trust him again, he'd have to earn it. That was fine by him. She was worth it. "I guess I'll see you tomorrow?"

He nodded, and after a silent moment, Angelle walked back to her waiting family. They immediately enclosed her in a circle of protection, and he caught snippets of her whiskey voice assuring them she was okay. That *they* were okay, just taking a breather. Even while knowing she was covering for their ruse, Cane hoped it was the truth. After she accepted a hug from her brothers and an all-too-eager ex, Angelle left the field with her family. Lacey and Eva flanked her on either side. She never once glanced back.

Cane stood there watching, regret threatening to swallow him whole. A throbbing ache pulsed in his chest. Fisting a hand, he rubbed the spot Angelle kissed moments before his life went to hell. Finally, when he got tired of the pitying looks from the lingering crowd, he began the trek to get his costume.

It was going to be a long day.

Chapter Sixteen

The sliding glass door of Holiday Inn opened and warm air hit Cane in the face. Hands empty because his luggage was still at Angelle's, he strode into the lobby. He'd driven aimlessly for twenty minutes—no real destination or goal in mind, other than giving Angelle space. Eventually he'd headed here, knowing he couldn't go back to her parents' house, and refusing to leave town again. He was staying, and he was going to fix this. How was still a mystery, but he had almost twenty-four hours to figure it out.

"Can I help you?"

Cane blinked, realizing he was standing like a mute jackass at the front desk. "Yeah," he answered, taking out his wallet. "I need a room."

Sliding his license and credit card onto the counter, Cane set his elbow on the edge and squeezed his temples. Lifeless green eyes and a broken smile stared from behind his eyelids. The signs of his handiwork. The taste of cherry lingered on his tongue. The scent of sunflowers laced with vanilla haunted him. And the sound of her voice rang in his ears: *Well, that beautiful heart is broken.*

Stabbing pain, every time.

An ache emanated from deep within his chest, not unlike when one of the guys in class threw him to the ground or caught him with a sucker-punch. His lungs felt restricted, like he couldn't draw a deep breath—but he'd be damned if he lost his shit in a Holiday Inn lobby. Scrubbing a hand over his face, Cane clamped his molars and stood up.

"Room 212, sir," the man said, sliding Cane his credit card, license, and room key. "Here's your key card, and your room's right off the elevator." He jutted his thumb behind him, and Cane mumbled his thanks.

The entire way up, he didn't see the elevator, or the plush carpet, or the long hall of rooms. He thought about her face as she walked away. Ever since he'd arrived in Bon Terre, Cane's life had been spinning out of control. He'd done the very things he'd sworn he would never do: he'd gotten attached, he'd let someone get too close, and then, he'd taken the heart of a good and loving woman, and crushed it.

Like father, like son.

His buzzing cell phone yanked Cane from memories of the past. Sliding his key card into the lock, he reached in his pocket with his free hand, hoping Angelle was calling. He didn't know what he'd say, but he wanted to hear her voice all the same. Yanking out his phone, he glanced at the screen, let out a breath, and opened the door. "What's up man?"

"Quick question about the wedding."

Jason's good-natured laugh rumbled over the other end, and despite his sour mood, Cane felt a smile tug at his lips. He tossed his keys and wallet onto the nightstand and fell onto the bed.

His sister was a wedding-obsessed nut. If it wasn't invitations, she was stressing over flower arrangements. She'd even made him suffer through a conversation over whether or not the men should wear a tie or a bowtie during the ceremony. For the record, Cane didn't care. As long as his sister's smile lit up the chapel, that's all that mattered.

Colby, however, saw things differently. And right now, Cane was grateful for the distraction. "What is it this time?" he asked.

"Colby's changed her mind, *again.*" The sound of a *slap*, no doubt from Colby swatting her fiancé's arm, snapped across the line, and Jason laughed. "Now it's the restaurant after the rehearsal. They need a final head count by tonight. It's just immediate family, but Colby thought you might want a plus one."

His sister's raised voice chimed in, "A certain redheaded fiancée, perhaps?"

And that distraction Cane had been so desperate for vanished.

Another matchmaking attempt. This was not what he needed right now. Jaw clenched, he counted to five then said, "The *restaurant* needed to know, huh?" Cane heard the undisguised frustration bleeding into his tone, but damn. "Maybe you can tell the restaurant to mind their damn business."

Jason made a noise in his throat, then he said, "Hang on a minute."

Cane heard him whisper to Colby followed by the sound of the television growing faint. A door clicked, and Jason's sharp tone came across the line. "All right, dude, chill out. I know your sisters are pushing the Angelle thing, but this is legit. The Court of Two Sisters had a cancelation. They can squeeze us in, but they need a firm head count. This is important to Colby, and I'm not going to let you jump all over her because you're in a pissy mood."

Cane scrubbed a hand over his face. Now he felt like an even bigger ass.

Colby's heart had been set on that restaurant from the beginning. It was where Jason had taken her on their first date. But after changing the wedding date to accommodate out of town guests and settling on the weekend before Christmas, they'd been booked solid by the time she'd made reservations.

"Shit. I'm sorry." Cane released a heavy breath. With his right hand, he squeezed his temples where he felt a headache coming on. "It's just been a bad morning."

"Don't sweat it." Jason's voice was back to easygoing, confirmation he was a better friend than Cane deserved. "It happens. But you know if you need to talk it out, I'm here. Hell, you'd be doing me a favor. Colby has us making gift baskets for out of town guests right now."

Cane chuckled, scratching the side of his jaw as he considered Jason's offer. As a rule, he dealt with his shit on his own. But at this point, what the hell did he have to lose?

"Ah, I screwed up with Angelle," he said, scrunching the pillow behind his head. "Shit happened, and now she hates me."

The phone went strangely silent. Then, "So did I catch you on the drive back home?"

Cane's restless foot stilled. "No," he admitted. "I checked into a Holiday Inn."

His best friend of more than thirty years laughed. He quickly covered it by clearing his throat, but he laughed. "Let me make sure I have this straight. The girl you've been trying to get with for half a year hates you. You're sticking around in a small town where no one knows you but her. And now you're alone in a hotel room, snapping my head off. Girls getting pissed at you is nothing new, but it bothers you that Angelle is." Jason's voice was thoroughly amused as he asked, "Did I get that right?"

Right here, *this* was exactly why guys didn't do the talking thing. Jase was lucky this conversation was happening over the damn phone. "Yeah, you got it. Now forget it. Just tell Colby I'll be home late tomorrow night, and no to the plus one, all right?"

He was seconds away from hanging up when he heard Jason say, "Hang on, man." Without really knowing why, Cane lifted the phone back to his ear. "You know I was just busting your chops. But damn, this girl's done a number on you, hasn't she?"

Cane huffed a breath. "Yeah, I guess she has."

"Do you have any idea how long I've waited for a woman to knock you on your ass?" When Cane didn't answer, Jason did for him. "Years. More than a decade. But the day Angelle walked into that diner, I knew it was just a matter of time."

Cane's headache pulsed between his eyebrows. "Did you miss the part where I said she hates me? Because she does. And it's probably better for her if it stays that way."

It was the truth. He wasn't throwing in the towel—he was in too deep to give up that easily. But even as he wanted Angelle to forgive him, he knew it'd be better for her if she didn't. He was a Robicheaux, after all.

Jason grunted. "That's a load of bullshit."

"Excuse me?"

"You heard me," he replied. "And I'll say it again. That was a load of bullshit, and I'll tell you why. It's not true. You like Angelle. A lot. But you're as stubborn as Colby. You think that if you let yourself care about this girl, *any* girl, you'll hurt her. That you'll cheat and break her down, just like your old man did to your mom. So you pushed her away. But you're not your dad, Cane. You wouldn't do what he did."

Jason's words released a flood of memories. They flashed and banged inside Cane's brain. The helplessness of hearing his mother cry in her room. The anger of hearing his dad on the phone with *her*. He'd seen the cracks in his mother's smile. Saw the pain she tried hiding from her family and friends. But

Cane had known the truth. And after things got better, when his parents had reconciled and Cane had forgiven his father, he never forgot. His mother went to her grave believing she'd kept her husband's infidelity and personal agony a secret. Cane would go to his remembering it.

Remembering was the only way he could make sure the cycle ended with him.

Cane closed his eyes. "I may be my own man, Jase, but you can't know that I'm any different. Hell, I already hurt Angelle. That's proof enough."

"Proof that you're human," Jason replied. "Relationships are real, man. They're messy. People screw up, they say asinine things, and then they suck it up, grovel, and move on. It comes with the territory. But the big stuff, like cheating? That doesn't. And even if it did, you're too stubborn to let it."

He wanted to believe what his friend was saying. And it did make sense. He'd like to think his mother's pain would be enough to keep him from ever doing the same thing. Even if it did, that didn't mean he'd be any good in a relationship. "Angelle can do better."

"You're kidding, right?" Jason exhaled into the phone. "You're an overprotective freak who puts the women you love on a pedestal. If you ever got your head out of your ass, you'd see you've had Angelle up there with Colby, Sherry, and Emma for months. It doesn't get any better than that."

Cane opened his eyes, followed by his mouth, prepared to tell Jason *his* head must be in his fiancée's ass. Cane didn't do love. Never been in it, and didn't plan on changing that. But when he went to say it aloud, the words wouldn't come.

One thing his friend had right? Cane was an overprotective freak. Angelle brought out that need unlike any woman he'd ever known. She also turned him on unlike any woman he'd ever met. Neither of those things had diminished after last night. They'd only grown stronger.

Angelle didn't need protection. She was tougher than she gave herself credit for. But he still wanted to be the one to keep her safe, from the world and from men like his father…men he'd feared he could be like. But as Cane's beliefs continued to realign, he realized Jason was right about another thing. He *wasn't* his father. And the reason he finally knew that was because no other woman could possibly tempt him away from his green-eyed hellcat.

"Shit."

Jason chuckled, but otherwise stayed quiet. Surprising, since he'd been full of hot air earlier. But damn if he hadn't been right.

"I love her." The words sounded strange rolling out of his mouth, but Cane knew it was the truth. *And she wants nothing to do with me.* "Why the hell didn't I know this before?"

"Because you're an idiot," his friend suggested, clearly enjoying this.

Cane again found himself wishing this chat were in person so Jason could see the obscene gesture he'd flipped him. But he wasn't mad at Jase—he was pissed at himself. Now that the foreign emotions clanging around in his chest made sense and he finally knew how he felt, panic was welling like a levee that had been breached.

"What if she doesn't forgive me?" he asked, more aloud to himself than for an answer.

"You make it so that she has to," Jason said, answering anyway. "And for added pressure, I'm putting you down for a plus one. Now you have no choice. Unless you want to owe me eighty bucks."

Cane shook his head, but damn if his heart wasn't pounding. He'd caught the Robicheaux love curse. Only with Angelle, it felt more like a boon.

"And hey, man, I'm sorry if I overstepped my bounds earlier," Jason said. "It's just you deserve what I found with

Colby, and for you, I think that's Angelle."

Smiling for the first time since he'd left her arms, Cane nodded. She *was* it for him. "No, we're good. I needed a kick in the ass." Then remembering Jason's earlier words he added, "Or my head taken out of it."

He didn't have a plan. Didn't know how he'd convince her to give them a real shot after what he did. But he'd figure it out. He had to. Cane wasn't *just* going to be Angelle's first. He was going to be her only. Her forever. She simply didn't know it yet.

When a knocking sound came from the other end, followed by Colby's muffled voice asking for the phone, Cane was still smiling. A matchmaking assault would be much easier to handle now. Maybe he'd even let his sister in on his latest discovery.

"Hey, big brother." As expected, Colby's tone definitely implied she was up to something. "I just got off the phone with Sherry, and she mentioned Angie sounded a little down."

He sat up, his smile beginning to fade. Could she have told Sherry what had happened? "She did?"

"I'm sure it's nothing," Colby assured him, allowing Cane to breathe easier. "Just if you can, try to make a big deal out of her birthday today, okay? Girls really love that."

The last of the smile on Cane's face died, along with any chance he had for forgiveness.

• • •

The posse was in full force. Everywhere Angelle looked in her mama's kitchen, a relative or friend was standing around, eager to offer a strained smile or wish her a happy birthday. The false cheer was like thousands of tiny little icepicks stabbing her brain. Bless their hearts, they all meant well. And she loved them for trying. But the last thing Angie wanted today was a freaking party.

"Never was one for birthdays, huh, Little Red?" Lacey pushed up onto the kitchen island, ignoring the empty seat in front of her, and handed Angie a cookie. Now *that* she could get behind. "Listen, I don't know what went down this morning between you and that handsome piece of fake fiancé beefcake. It seemed major, and you both looked miserable. But you know if you need me to, I'm willing to scrap."

Angelle bit into her much needed chocolate fix as her cousin lifted her arms, flexed her lean biceps, then ducked to press a kiss on each.

Eyes alight with humor, Lacey declared, "With these bad boys, I can totally take him. Even if he is bigger than Goliath."

Angie rested her head on her cousin's lap, grateful for the gentle teasing. No one had a clue why she and Cane were on the outs—no one other than maybe her parents, that is. Even with Lacey's behind-the-scenes info, the truth was too embarrassing for Angelle to admit. So instead, she'd been vague all day, knowing how bad she was at lying. She'd said they'd had a disagreement, which was true—she disagreed with his choice to leave her naked and alone in a loft. And that they were taking time off to think, another truth. All Angelle had done today was think. Think about why Cane had shown up. She'd been so sure he'd taken off after getting what he wanted. She'd thought about the dozens of unanswered questions swirling in her mind. Questions she could've had answered that morning, had she not been too afraid to hear them.

If the choices were drive herself insane with thinking, have family members walk on eggshells around her, or let her cousin distract her with crazy antics, Angie definitely chose the latter.

Lacey combed her fingers through Angelle's hair. "No one messes with my baby cousin."

Taking a breath, Angelle sat back up. "Eighteen months and three days older, Lace. Any chance we can drop the baby?"

When a flash of guilt crossed her face, she nudged Lacey's knee to show she was teasing. Because she was. *Mostly.* She knew that none of the pet names really meant anything. They were just habit. A pattern the town had fallen into over the years, and she'd allowed it. But those names only reinforced the idea that Angelle was weak. Hopeless. And she wasn't. If nothing else, Cane had taught her that.

She had an inner hellcat.

"Consider it done. But girl, you know I didn't mean nothing, right?" Lacey's bright red lips pursed in a frown, one that lifted when Angelle nodded around another bite of cookie. "Good. Because believe me, with the way that beefcake looks at you? No one's confused on that issue. It's pretty obvious that since you left Bon Terre you've become *all* woman…if you know what I mean."

The way Lacey's head bobbed up and down, a knowing smirk on her face and crude noises emitting from her throat, Angie was sure even young Sadie would know what she meant.

Angelle shook her head, feeling her lips twitch despite the emotional storm raging inside her chest. Growing up, her cousin had been her closest confidante and the next best thing to her very own Dr. Ruth. Lacey was just as sex-crazed as Sherry. Angie's continued "hymenally challenged" state after eight years with Brady had been a frequent topic, so it shouldn't be a surprise now. But with the status change so recent, and Angelle's complete lack of a poker face, there was no fighting back the smile.

She dropped her gaze to the countertop, but she wasn't fast enough.

Cackling, Lacey thrust a finger in Angelle's chest. "I *knew* it! Spill your guts, woman. I need details, stat!"

Angie actually laughed. A feat only Lacey could manage on a day as sucky as this one. "Lord, I've missed you," she said, smiling at her cousin while skillfully avoiding the topic at hand. "You have to come visit me in Magnolia Springs. Just remind me to hide my roommate when you do, because I don't think the town's big enough for the two of you."

Lacey handed her a second cookie from the plate and winked. "Deal, but only if you introduce me to a hunky firefighter or two while I'm there."

"You got it."

They tapped cookies in agreement, and Angie took another huge bite. One benefit of her birthday misery was the unlimited snackage. Cookies, cake, ice cream, comfort foods. If everyone could leave her alone with her riches, she'd be halfway to the ultimate breakup cure. Add in *Sisterhood of the Traveling Pants* and a box of tissues, and she'd be good to go.

"Now there's the smile I remember."

At the sound of her ex's voice, Angelle and Lacey exchanged a glance. What began as sweet, friendly behavior this morning was bordering on annoying. Brady's doting left no question—in anyone's minds—that he wanted to get back together. Even more obvious was the division her family and friends had taken concerning the two men in her life.

Two men.

Ha! More like zero men. Brady was great, but he didn't make her heart jump. As for Cane, he'd broken her heart, but she couldn't deny he'd made the shards shake when she saw him. She'd been so sure he was out of her life—if he'd ever really been in it to begin with. But after his shocking appearance at the park that morning, he was one big question mark.

It seemed the only thing *not* under question was Lacey's

position. She was firmly on team Cane. So when a sly grin curved her lips and she glanced at Brady, Angelle knew she was up to something.

"Yep," she said, "I knew I could make Angie smile. All I had to bring up was—"

"How much I love chocolate!"

Wide-eyed, Angelle shot Lacey a look. As crazy as the woman was, she didn't *think* her cousin would actually disclose the details of her sex life to her ex…but with Lacey, you just never knew. The mischievous smile she bit off was proof of that.

Brady's head slanted, his eyebrows furrowed, as telltale warmth flooded Angelle's cheeks. Yep, she was as bad a liar as ever. Luckily, the *ding* of the doorbell kept her from making it worse. Jumping to her feet, she exclaimed, "I'll get it!"

With a released breath, she scooted into the hall, the words *saved by the bell* running through her head. But as she got closer and closer to the front door, her eager footsteps slowed.

What if it was Cane at the door?

The thought both terrified and excited her.

Rubbing damp hands on the rough denim of her jeans, Angelle wondered what she'd say if it was. At the park, she'd let fear get the best of her. After she woke up alone, she'd tried convincing herself that she no longer loved him, that it'd been too soon, and his leaving destroyed any tender feelings she may've had. But the second she'd spotted him, dark circles sitting like half-moons under his eyes, dark hair mussed and jaw in need of a shave, she'd known just how bad of a liar she really was.

Lacey was right—he *had* looked miserable. Almost as miserable as her, which didn't make any sense. He was the one who had left. When she went to return his ring, it had devastated her. It was like giving up on a dream that she hadn't quite admitted to until that morning. But then Cane had refused to accept it.

Was it possible he did care for her, and this was one huge misunderstanding?

It appeared as though she was about to find out.

Angelle closed her eyes, shook out her hands, and whispered, "I'm a hellcat." Then with her shoulders back, she strode forward and tugged open the solid door.

It wasn't Cane. Unless he'd shrunk, de-aged about fifteen years, and developed a wicked case of acne. The teenager in front of her was a stranger, an oddity around Bon Terre, and in his arms was a huge bouquet of flowers, a rectangular box in which she spotted the word *chocolate*, and a tutu-wearing teddy bear. Not a total replica of the one she'd given Sadie, but darn close.

Tears that had been sitting under the surface, just waiting for an excuse to come out, sprang to her eyes. It might not have been Cane at the door, but she felt his presence as strongly as if it were.

"Angelle Prejean?" the young man asked, shifting the flowers so he could read the name on the bright white envelope inside.

Hand over her mouth to contain a sob, Angie nodded. Through the slats of her fingers she said, "That's me."

"Awesome." He thrust the flowers forward as the sound of nearing footsteps echoed behind her. Lacey arrived in time to accept the teddy bear and box of chocolate-covered cherries. Removing a clipboard from his bag, he asked, "Can you sign this?"

Lacey made a move to take the flowers, but Angelle tightened her grip. Sunflowers were her favorite, and the fact that Cane knew that made her chest ache. Holding that bulging vase of sunflowers, roses, and lilies was the closest thing she had to him, and right now, she needed it. Angie shifted the weight to her left side and quickly scrawled her name on the paper.

With a two-fingered salute, the teenager said, "Later," and hoofed it back to his truck.

"The beefcake has interesting taste in teddy bear ensembles, but he gets mad points for the chocolate." Lacey lifted the plastic-wrapped box to her nose like she could smell the contents, then admired the bouquet. "And those flowers are freaking gorgeous. What's the card say?"

Angelle shrugged, biting her lip as she swiped at the tears on her cheeks. "I don't know. I'm kind of scared to read it," she admitted. *Hellcats can be nervous sometimes, can't they?*

"Well, I'm not." Lacey set the bear and the chocolates on the entryway table. "Let me at it."

Reaching into the middle of the large bouquet, her cousin snatched the envelope. It was thicker, bulkier than normal. Lacey lifted an eyebrow and cracked the seal, turning the card over to release a bottle cap in her palm. Handing it to Angie she said, "This guy is either completely nuts, or you're perfect for each other."

Angelle didn't reply. She was too busy being flabbergasted. It was the second bottle cap from the night they babysat. She'd kept hers, but had misplaced the other one before they left. Or at least that's what she'd thought. Now she knew he'd taken it. Closing her hand around the surprising memento, Angelle's broken heart pulsed.

Lacey cleared her throat. "Angel," she read, "I know I promised to give you space. Sorry if this is breaking the rules. In case you're wondering, these items aren't random. They're just a small sample of things that make me think of you. Sunflowers, cherries, even pansy teddy bears. You can keep this one, but the bottle cap is mine. It's on loan, a memory from a very special night, and I'll need it back."

Her cousin looked up and said, "Yep, perfect for each

other."

"Keep reading!" Angelle wiped at the continued tears, needing to hear more.

With a smile, Lacey read, "Happy Birthday, angel. I'm counting the hours until we talk. Yours, Cane." So his sister had spilled the beans after all. As Angelle pondered how long he'd known, her cousin slid the card back into the envelope and said, "If you don't want him, let me know. I'll gladly mend his broken heart."

Angelle knew she was teasing, but it really wasn't a question of wanting. She knew, despite everything, she still wanted Cane more than she'd wanted anything in her life. What she had to figure out, however, was if that was enough. And if she could ever trust him again.

Chapter Seventeen

It would figure that on the day Cane volunteered to wear a borrowed polyester Santa suit and a scratchy as hell fake beard the weather would be unseasonably warm. Like over eighty degrees warm. As if mentally sweating his conversation with Angelle weren't enough, now he was physically sweating, too. It was a good thing he was a sucker for kids. And hot redheads.

Chucking a handful of candy canes at the two boys perched on their fathers' shoulders, Cane hummed along to "Walking in a Winter Wonderland." It was the second time he'd heard the tune that morning. The truck pulling his pirogue sleigh (along with the eight stuffed alligators, obviously) was blaring a playlist of Christmas songs on repeat. He was at the very end of the procession with only a fire truck behind him, its sole purpose being to signal with a loud, occasional *beep beep* that they'd reached the end of the parade. Well, its purpose was that, and to feed his mounting tension headache.

As he tossed another handful into the crowd, this time plastic beads with Christmas trees, he shouted, "Ho-ho-ho."

The irony that this whole journey began with him saying the same words in a similar get-up at the Bachelor Auction was not lost on him. He still felt ridiculous, but this time he didn't mind so much. He was doing it for the woman he loved.

The procession stalled, and Cane sat back in his Christmas tree throne. He'd only seen Angelle once, a brief glimpse when they were all lining up. But it had been enough to stop his heart. She was so damn beautiful it made his chest hurt. Since she'd given up her Cracklin Queen title, she didn't join the other women in the back of a convertible, smiling and waving like Miss America. This year she'd traded the smooth ride for water bottle duty with one of the dance teams. He'd watched from his last place position as she took her spot with the young girls, willing her to look at him. It wasn't as if he'd been hard to miss. But she hadn't. And that had made his anxiety about their talk skyrocket.

With a slight jerk, his float crept forward.

Smiling at the families gathered on Main Street, Cane wondered what Angelle had thought about his gifts. Other than his sisters and Emma, he'd never bought a woman gifts—and even for them, he tended to go with gift cards. But if he'd learned anything from the multitude of women in his life, it was that you can never go wrong with flowers and chocolate. At least that's what he'd thought, but even that had taken forever. He'd argued with three different florists. Ran to that damn bear shop in the packed mall before searching shelves at Target for chocolates. And he'd debated forever about the bottle cap.

Did she get the significance? Should he have written *Love, Cane* on the card?

Chick thoughts. That's what his mental process had been reduced to. But he figured as long as the result involved Angelle being in his arms, he could deal with being whipped.

Another cycle or two through the eclectic Christmas mix,

his role as Papa Noel was over. Back at the civic center, away from impressionable children's eyes, Cane yanked off the scratchy beard. After shucking the pillows used for jelly-belly stuffing, and removing the Santa hat and hair, he raked a hand through his own. Reaching back, he stripped off his soaked T-shirt and used it as a towel before throwing the coat back on.

Marching bands continued to play for fun as he made his way through a maze of horses, buggies, and floats made to look like old homes on the bayou, combing the area for Angelle. As hurt and angry as she was, he knew she'd stick around. More than likely with a Brady-sized shadow. That man was campaigning hard for a second chance. Too damn bad. Cane would wear that damn Santa suit for the rest of his life before he'd let that happen.

When the toy train float drove off, he finally found her. She was standing near the gazebo, and as expected, Brady was by her side.

"There you are." He couldn't help the smug grin that formed, seeing her step away from her ex as she turned to face Cane. That grin grew as her gaze slid appreciatively over his opened coat and bare chest. Good to see she wasn't immune. "Enjoy the parade?"

Angelle nodded, shoving a thick section of auburn hair behind her ear. "And you?"

"I did." He darted an annoyed glance at Brady, then stepped forward and took her hand. She visibly tensed but she didn't yank it back, and Cane counted that a victory. "Ready to talk?"

"Yeah." Rocking back on her heels, she turned to Brady and said, "See you at the Fais Do Do?"

A muscle in the man's jaw ticked, but he nodded. "I'll be there. But if you want me to, I can stick around until you're done. In case you need me."

Hell if that didn't set off a firestorm in Cane's blood. The only man Angelle needed was *him*. Cane was proving that today—to her, to her family, to the whole damn town. And if he had to go through the good doctor to do that, so be it. But before he could go off on the man, Angelle's thumb snaked out of Cane's grasp to squeeze his. The pulse brought his attention back to her. Back where it belonged.

"Go home, Brady," she said, deep green eyes staring into his. "I'm good here."

Those three words were like a balm. Cane hoped they were also a clue to how the conversation would go, what she was thinking. He held tight to her hand, waiting as Brady finally strolled away. Then tugging her toward the bench seat, he asked, "Did you get my gifts?"

Angelle sat beside him, a small smile curving her mouth. "Yes, I did. And I loved them." Relief washed over him, but it was unfortunately short-lived. "But I don't understand them."

Cane watched as Angelle's shoulders dropped and her face pinched. Her chin trembled as she reached inside her pocket with her free hand and pulled out two bottle caps—the one he'd given her, plus her own. He'd assumed she had kept hers, as she said she would. But seeing them side by side in her perfect, shaking palm stole his breath.

He wasn't letting her leave the gazebo without putting it all on the line. Everything. He was in, 100 percent.

"Help me understand," she said, her voice wobbly and full of the hurt he'd caused. "Why do all of this, the presents, the sticking around, the wanting to talk, if you don't care? And if you *do*, then why did you leave? Because that *crushed*—" Her whiskey voice broke, sending a fresh batch of self-loathing to his gut. She sucked in her lips, swallowed, and tried again. "It crushed me to wake up alone and realize I was just another conquest. Another notch on your belt. And seeing you yesterday, seeing you now, getting your gifts…it crushes me all over again. I'm never gonna get over it—over *you*—if you keep coming around. Is that what you want?"

"Yes." Her mouth tumbled open, eyes shocked at his admission, and he explained. "I don't want to cause you any additional pain. That's the last thing I want. But I don't want you getting over me. I want you *under* me," he said, unable to help himself, "and I want you next to me. I want you holding my hand in a gazebo and sitting next to me on the couch. I want you."

Angelle looked away, her eyebrows furrowed as she shook her head. "I'm so confused."

She was adorable, even in the middle of a heartbreak. If she hadn't completely owned his heart before this moment, she did now. Gently steering her chin back so she faced him, Cane dared to press a kiss against her forehead before saying, "Then let me try to explain."

He took a deep breath and waited for her nod to continue. "I push people away. It's what I do. I keep them at a safe distance because that way I know I can't hurt them. I don't let people in or let them see what a nerd I am. Angel, I love crossword puzzles. And Sudoku. I watch far too much Discovery channel and I wear glasses when I read, which I also do a lot."

The squiggle on Angelle's forehead vanished as her lips tipped up in a smile. The tears had stopped, too, and Cane counted that his second victory.

"I know I hurt you by leaving," he told her. "You have to know I've regretted it every second since. Angelle, you make me feel things I never have before. I didn't know how to handle it, so I fell back on my normal response." Cane looked away, unable to meet her eyes when he admitted, "I pushed you away."

Angelle had the biggest heart of anyone he'd ever known. Where he pushed, she pulled. Could a person as good and loving as she was understand his actions?

"And how *do* I make you feel?"

At her soft question, he looked back. Angelle blushed, her cheeks turning a beautiful shade of pink as she fidgeted with the bottle caps in her hand. Cane closed his hand around hers, waiting until she lifted her eyes to say, "You broke through every wall I put up. I can't push you away because you're already in. Not just in my heart, angel. You're in my soul."

And then, he waited.

He didn't breathe, didn't think, didn't look away. Cane watched Angelle as she processed his words, internalized them. And when her eyes glimmered, he watched as she began to believe them. Or at least he hoped that was what the fresh tears meant.

"This week has been the best of my life, but it was built around a lie. Our relationship, while real in so many ways, was a hoax. I want more. I want a *real* chance. A real relationship with you." He brushed away a tear that fell down her cheek, pausing to gather his nerve to ask the question burning a hole in his chest. "Have I completely blown my shot?"

She closed her eyes, effectively shutting him out from what she was thinking. That was his first warning sign. But it wasn't until she slowly drew her hands away from his and brought them both to her head that the real panic set in. "Angel?"

"I'm sorry." The two words he did *not* want to hear. Opening her eyes, she shifted on the bench, turning her body to face him. "My head is all over the place right now. I want to say yes. I want to jump in and say, let's do this. But another part of me says run for the hills. You hurt me badly," she told him, not sugarcoating it. "I heard everything you said. It was beautiful, and I want to trust that you believe it, that you meant it. But this is just coming at me so fast."

Cane swallowed hard, rooted to his spot. Nothing existed

in that moment but him and Angelle. Her conflicted eyes riveted him, even as they tore at his heart.

Licking her lips, she ran a frazzled hand through her hair. "The old me would jump. That's what you want, and I want to make you happy. I want to believe that you can make *me* happy. But I've always put other people's needs before my own. Now, I'm finally standing on my own two feet, and Cane, you helped that happen. I don't want to backpedal." Angelle's lips pursed when his body stiffened, and she took his hands in hers. "I'm not explaining myself well. I'm not saying no."

Cane's heart began beating again.

"I'm saying…can I have some time? To just think this through? When I give you my answer, I want us both to know that I'm not acting blindly or doing what I think you want me to do, but doing what *I* want to do. Can I have that?"

How could he say no? He couldn't. But damn, did he want to.

Cane glanced at his watch. "The Fais Do Do begins at six. That's four hours. Is that enough time?"

Angelle's lips pressed together in a half-grimace, half-smile and she said, "Yeah. That should be good."

Nodding, he pushed to his feet. "Then I guess I'll leave you to it." Cane tugged his keys from the pocket of his Santa pants, trying to hold on to some semblance of optimism. The battle wasn't over. He hadn't lost. He had to trust the glimmer of love he still saw in her eyes, which had grown bigger the more they spoke.

And if he did that, then it meant Cane had a stop to make before he returned to the hotel.

"You need a ride home?" he asked, for more than just the obvious reason.

She shook her head, releasing a heavy breath. "No, I drove Mama's car here. Besides, I think I'm gonna cut a block." When he raised his eyebrows, her conflicted smile widened.

"Drive around for a while. It helps me think."

Cane nodded again, turning to make the trek back to his truck. At the entrance to the gazebo, he knocked his fist against the wood and looked over his shoulder. "Angel?" She lifted her head and he said, "You should know that I don't plan to give up easily."

• • •

Where is he?

Angelle glanced at her watch for the bazillionth time since arriving at the civic center. Two minutes had passed since she'd last looked. Two minutes in which Cane still hadn't shown up. It was now six thirty. Thirty minutes *after* the Fais Do Do started, and twenty-nine minutes and fifty-nine seconds after she'd begun her relentless obsession of staring at the entrance. Seriously, where was he?

The jostling table snapped her focus away from the door, and her gaze collided with Brady's.

"A smart man knows when he's been beaten," he announced, his lips pressed together in a defeated frown. Angelle winced, and he nudged her elbow, his mouth morphing into a self-deprecating grin. "It's for the best. I knew it was a long shot, but I had to try. You're an amazing woman, Angie, and I'm sorry if I didn't let you know that enough."

"We just had bad timing. Maybe if we'd met now, after you'd finished school and were living here full time…" Angelle's voice trailed off. He crooked an eyebrow, waiting for her to finish, and she propped her chin on her hand. "You know what? I don't know if that's true. See, Brady, I think the girl you loved, the type of girl you need, is the one I tried to be. That's not anything you did," she quickly added, watching as a shadow fell over his face. "I did it to myself. You never got to know the real me, because I never let her out. Heck, I didn't even know her."

As Brady's eyes grew more confused, Angelle's widened in realization. Huh. She and Cane were a lot more alike than she'd ever realized. He hid his true self away, not wanting anyone to get close because he was afraid of hurting people. She hid *her* true self away, not wanting anyone to get close because she was afraid of disappointing people. Of doing or saying the wrong thing, of making a mistake. But all she'd done was hurt herself. Just like Cane, who kept himself from experiencing true love and real relationships.

They were both so screwed up. And they were perfect for each other.

She'd already decided that, about five minutes into her drive that afternoon. She was still glad she'd asked for the time, though. It was a good first step. Something she'd never tried before. And thanks to that drive, Angie knew, with every fiber of her being, that she wanted that real chance with Cane.

She glanced at the entrance. Still no Cane.

"Well, I loved the Angie I knew," Brady said, leaning forward on his elbows. "And I look forward to getting to know this new you, too. As friends, obviously," he added, raising his palms off the table.

The band began a toe-tapping beat, and Angelle had energy to burn. "You were my best friend for a quarter of my life. I'd like to think you'll stay that way." She smiled, and he returned it. "And your first act of friendship with the new and improved me is asking me to dance. Cane's not here yet and I'm going stir-crazy. I need a distraction."

Pushing back his chair, he stood and held out his hand. "Now, that I can do."

Brady kept his word, distracting Angelle through two fast-tempo songs. Twirling around, getting lost in the rhythm of the music, it felt like home. She'd always been herself on the dance floor. Stomping her foot, Angie sang along with the chorus, deciding she'd find a local chapter of the Cajun French Music Association when she returned to Magnolia Springs. Brady twirled her a final time, and then as the song ended, they broke apart to clap with the crowd.

As Angelle chanced a glance around the room, a slow two-step began.

"Still not here?" Brady asked, shoving his hands in his pockets. Couples danced around them as Angie shook her head. "We can keep dancing, if you want." His mouth kicked up in a good-natured smile. "No funny business, I promise."

After only a slight hesitation, she agreed. It seemed more and more as though Cane wasn't coming at all. Déjà vu swirled in her stomach. He wouldn't ditch her two days in a row, would he? After what he'd proclaimed a few short hours ago? Brady twirled her around the floor a few times, her eyes constantly seeking the figures standing along the periphery of the room. But his tall, well-built frame was never among them.

Somewhere around their fourth rotation, he said, "Love looks good on you, Angie."

Angelle lifted her head rather suddenly, confused. "Where did that come from?"

Brady chuckled. "I know you loved me once, but that started changing a long time ago. I didn't want to admit it, but I knew. But even on our best days, in the beginning of our relationship, you never looked at me the way you look at Cane. I think that's why I acted the way I did the last couple days. I wanted that."

Angelle opened her mouth to say…she didn't know what. Maybe to apologize. Maybe to tell him he'd find that soon. But he shook his head and said, "I also want to look at a woman the way Cane looks at you. I never gave you that, and I'm happy you finally found it."

"I'm not so sure about that," she mumbled, feeling and

sounding completely bitter. She may as well admit it aloud. "I thought he felt the same way, but obviously he doesn't. He's not here, is he?"

"Yeah he is," Brady said, smiling as he looked past her shoulder. "I'm staring at the man right now, and that look is all over his face."

Angelle turned just as the music came to an abrupt end. Cane smiled, shrugging from his place behind the microphone, a guitar strapped to his chest. "Sorry everybody."

Couples began whispering on the crowded dance floor, several of them pointing or smiling at her as they realized who the city boy was on the stage. Cane spoke with the members of the band, who nodded and shook his hand, then he turned back, locking eyes with Angelle.

Her heart began a wild rhythm, faster than any Zydeco beat she'd ever heard.

Oh my God.

"I know this is a Fais Do Do," he told the crowd, "but I don't know any Cajun songs. I know, shocker, right? But see, there's a woman in the audience who needs to know how I feel, and I do that best in song. Now, I realize that's kind of a cop-out," he said with a smirk, fingering the chords on his guitar, "so first I'll tell you a little about my hellcat."

Lacey appeared beside her out of nowhere, grabbing her hand and squeezing it tight. "Eep," she whispered. Angelle nodded. *Eep* was right.

"I've never been in love before," Cane announced to the crowd, eliciting a round of *aw*s from the women. He grinned and said, "Before I met her, that is." Angelle's mouth fell open, her breathing stopped. "So when I started to fall, I didn't realize it. It wasn't one of those 'love at first sight' things, like you see in the movies. For us, it started with a woman tripping over her feet in a diner, and looking at me as if I was a hoodlum trying to steal her purse."

He strummed some more as people chuckled. Angelle felt like she was having an out of body experience. Was this really happening? Lacey squeezed her hand again, proving that it was.

One of the band members brought Cane a stool and he thanked him, settling back and propping his guitar on his thigh. Angelle had heard him play a few times, and it'd always been hard pretending she wasn't affected. Now she could openly swoon…as if she wasn't already.

Nimble fingers picked at the strings, a slow, romantic melody casting a spell over the crowd. Over her. "I realize I'm a little late tonight, but I was busy writing a song for my girl, so I hope this makes up for it." Cane smiled, the breathtaking one with the dimple, and Angie's heart nearly burst, it felt so full. "Angelle Prejean, this is for you."

Then, with a room full of her family and friends watching, Cane Robicheaux began singing a song, a song he wrote for her.

"It took me awhile to figure out, just who I was. But no matter how hard I try, she'll always be, the better half of us." He never looked at his hands as his smooth voice washed over her. His eyes stayed on hers, singing every lyric like it was a promise. The tears that had been welling in her eyes spilled over.

"I don't know what a man like me ever did to deserve her love. But I won't let her go. Lord, I need her so much, 'cause she's the better half of us."

Angelle heard Lacey sniffling beside her, but she didn't look away. She couldn't—she was spellbound. As Cane sang the following words, *"She's the very best part of me. Don't even wanna think about who I'd be, without her by my side,"* she could've sworn her bad boy choked up. *"So I'm swallowin' my pride, and I'm telling her tonight."*

Dark brown eyes full of love and sincerity drilled into

hers from across the room as he sang, *"You're the one I want to wake up to, the one I want to lay down at night. You're my little hellcat, in an angel's disguise."*

Any part of her heart and soul he hadn't already owned waved a white flag in protest. This beautiful man was pouring out his heart in front of a mesmerized audience, and the sincerity in his voice left no room for doubt.

She'd fallen for her fake fiancé, and he'd fallen right back.

His strumming slowed, and under the bright light above him, Angie saw the thick knot in Cane's throat bob as he swallowed. *"If it takes a lifetime, to earn back your trust, I'll die tryin' to make you see, you're the better half of us."* The music stopped, and it was just his voice and soulful eyes reaching out to her as he sang, *"Girl, you'll always be, the better half of us."*

Applause erupted when he finished, his chest heaving as he searched her eyes for an answer. When he pushed to his feet and strode purposefully across the floor, his devilish grin growing with each step, the crowd's cheers grew louder. And as he yanked Angelle into his arms and smashed his mouth against hers, they went ballistic.

The love and intensity Cane poured into this kiss overwhelmed her. Her head spun as his fingers speared through her hair, and he licked the seam of her lips, demanding more. Clinging to his shoulders, she gave everything she had, kissing him back with every ounce of love she had for him. It didn't matter that they were in the middle of the dance floor in front of people who'd seen her in diapers. This was her moment. And she was going to enjoy the heck out of it.

A noise rumbled in Cane's chest. Slowing the kiss, his hands loosened their grip around her. Fingertips grazed the skin on her arms as he lifted his head. Dark eyes full of passion that no longer scared her searched hers as they both caught their breath.

"I know I'm going to screw up. A lot. But I promise you, I'll never stop trying." He kissed her again and said, "I'm in love with you, angel."

Bursting. That's what it felt like her heart was doing as she rose onto her tiptoes and wrapped her arms around his neck. "That's all I need, Cane," she told him, hoping he could see how much she meant it. "The rest we'll figure out together. I love you. The *real* you."

Cane closed his eyes and exhaled, minty breath fanning her face. "Those are now my three favorite words," he said, pressing his forehead against hers as he looked into her eyes. "And I'm glad you agree because, angel, I have a question I need to ask you."

Anxiety etched the hard planes of his face. The entire animal kingdom set up shop in her gut, flying, dancing, and kicking as Angelle watched, completely awestruck, as the man she loved dropped to one knee.

Then, he slid his mother's ring off her finger.

Huh?

"The first time I put this ring on your finger, I did it wrong," he said, winking as he carefully chose his words for their rapt audience. "This time, everything is going to be perfect. You're it for me, angel. The words in that song, I meant them. No matter what happens, I won't let you go. I need you too damn much. I'm in. All in. And this afternoon I officially received your father's permission to ask…Angelle Elizabeth Prejean, will you marry me?" With a grin, he lowered his voice and added, "For real?"

Laughter and tears erupted at the same time. Her knees gave out and she went with it, throwing her arms around his neck and pressing kisses all over his face. "Yes. Yes. Yes," she said in between each one. "I love you, Cane Randall Robicheaux. And I can't wait to show you how much every day for the rest of our lives." She kissed him again, then held out her left hand and wiggled her fingers as she teased, "Now give me my ring back."

Cane laughed, a deep rumbling sound that made Angelle shiver. The handsome, sexy, reformed playboy smiling at her with love in his eyes was hers. And as he slid his mother's ring onto her finger, returning it to where it was meant to be, she gazed right back, knowing she'd finally found her forever.

Epilogue

Boudin balls, fresh cracklin, and Colby's beignets. For anyone else, that particular culinary trifecta might be an odd choice for a special dinner, but Cane Robicheaux was far from ordinary. He was her surprisingly sentimental, rugged city boy. And tonight, she was pulling out all the stops.

Nerves had her tummy doing backflips. It was too soon for it to be anything else. But in a few short months, she'd begin feeling flutters, and then bruising kicks, as the new life she and Cane had created grew inside her. Angelle still couldn't believe it.

Withholding the news from Colby and Sherry when they'd stopped by earlier had been nearly impossible, but her husband had to be the first to know. She loved his sisters like they were her own, but neither was very good at keeping secrets. Especially not ones like this. The Robicheaux clan had grown like crazy in the last year—adding husbands, wives, and adorable, preteen stepchildren. And now their numbers were increasing again.

I'm gonna be a mama!

The flash of a headlight and rumble of an engine sent Angelle's heart galloping into her throat. Cane was home. She flicked a thick slat in the blinds and watched her husband dismount from his bike. Twelve months together, five of them married, and he still turned her insides to goo.

She listened to the heavy clomp of motorcycle boots on the driveway, then dashed to the entry to let in her husband. Cane's eyes widened as she threw open the door.

"Eager to see me, darlin'?" he asked, flashing the pair of dimples that melted her every stinking time. He swooped her into his arms and lowered his head, eyes sparking with mischief as he said, "If I'd known you were this hot to see me, I'd have come home early."

Then Angie was lost in the power of Cane Robicheaux. His lips, his scent, the undeniable love that radiated from his fingertips into her heated skin. She was so far gone that he'd carried her halfway down the hall before she remembered her important news and, reluctantly, broke away from his kiss.

Cane frowned, and it was so adorable she couldn't help but laugh. Which, of course, only made his frown deepen. "Am I missing something?"

"No," she replied, sliding down his strong body and wrapping her arms around his waist. "You're most definitely not missing anything. You're quite equipped." Teasing and flirting with the man she loved was easy now. Not so much because she thought she was any good at it, but because being around her husband, seeing herself in his eyes, made her feel sexy. Confident. Like the woman he'd always thought her to be. "We *will* be coming back to that train of thought very soon. But first, I have a surprise for you."

Taking his hand in hers, she led him back to the kitchen where their banquet awaited. Cane eyed the offering with an amused quirk of his eyebrow. "Interesting selection. All my favorites." He popped a cracklin in his mouth and grinned. "So good." After chewing and swallowing, he tore a fluffy section of beignet, dipped it into the excess powdered sugar on the platter, then stuffed it, too, into his mouth. "Is today an anniversary of a first of something I'm forgetting? If so, I'm sorry, darlin! Men have crap for brains when it comes to that kind of stuff."

Angelle bit her lip, trying to contain her excitement. "It's the beginning of one," she answered, trying to draw out the mystery. Reaching under the table, she grabbed the present she'd hidden there earlier and slid it onto the table. Cane's eyebrow lifted even higher.

"For me?" Curiosity and excitement warred on his handsome face—he was such a sucker for presents. She nodded, holding her breath as he tore into the wrapping paper, and when two pairs of tiny socks, one pink and one blue, emerged in his large, calloused hands, she released it in one big burst.

The thick knot in Cane's throat bobbed as he swallowed. But other than that, zero reaction.

"I'm pregnant," Angelle told him, her voice wobbly, unsure of how to take his silence. "Only with one, that I know of, but they were both so cute I decided to get one of each." His eyes remained glued to the small garments of cotton, and she shoved a section of hair behind her ear, rocking back on her heels. "Are you happy?" she asked. "Completely freaking out? I can't tell what's going on in that giant analytical noggin of yours."

A shuddered breath escaped his parted lips. "Happy?" His dark brown eyes finally met hers, and Angelle saw they were misty. "Angel, from the day you agreed to be mine for real, I didn't think I could be any happier. Then I watched you walk down the aisle toward me and your father put your hand in mine, and I thought *that* was the happiest moment of my life. But this? Making me a father? Baby, you just rocked my world."

Seeing how much he meant his words, that he wanted this baby as much as she did, loosened something in her chest and Angelle's knees buckled. Cane caught her easily, pulling her close and supporting her weight like he'd supported *her* for the last year. Strong, unconditionally, and with surprising tenderness.

Cupping her cheek with his hand, he gently traced her freckles with the pad of his thumb. "It's just gonna keep getting better and better, isn't it?" he asked, ducking down to lean his forehead against hers. "You've made me happier than I ever knew I could be, Angelle Robicheaux."

Angie stared into her husband's eyes, loving how unguarded they were. He was hers, all of him. The math nerd, the inked-up bad boy, and every shade in between. "And I'm the luckiest woman on the face of the earth, Cane Robicheaux," she replied, closing her eyes as she pressed a kiss against his lips. "Taking a chance on you was the best decision I ever made."

That naughty glint entered his eyes again, and he scooped her into his arms, grinning wider as she squealed. Cradling her against his chest, he lowered his mouth and said against her lips, "You got that right." Then he took her to their bedroom, celebratory dinner postponed for now, and proceeded to show her just how lucky she was.

Acknowledgments

So much of an author's day is spent staring at a blank screen, talking with imaginary friends, and scaring innocent people in Panera when you unconsciously act out the scenes you are writing. Or is that just me? Anyhoo, I've made so many friends along this journey, authors, bloggers, reviewers, and readers who lift me up, cheer me on, and virtually bop me over the head when I eventually lapse into the completely random and silly. For everyone listed below, and for everyone my chaotic author/mama brain forgot (and will be kicking myself over in 3, 2, 1…), I hope you know that I adore you all to pieces.

First up, I have to thank my beautiful cousin, Chantel Fouchi, for the fabulous tour of Cajun country and letting me take over your home for a week—sorry about the ceiling! Your friends and neighbors were so kind and welcoming, and it's their stories that gave this book life. Like Cane, I'm New Orleans Cajun, so this city girl needed some schooling. And they totally brought it. Ryan and Mary Rose Verret gave the Prejean family a heart. The Marcantel and Coleman families welcomed me into their homes and inspired so much of the

Bon Terre townspeople's stories. Tony Thibodeaux introduced me to the buggy capital of the world, and Dexter Thibodeaux taught me about cutting blocks, Thanksgiving traditions, and Johnny Janot. If this book sparked your curiosity for Cajun culture, listening to Janot's song "I'm Proud to be a Cajun" is a must!

Ashley Bodette, assistant extraordinaire, rocks my socks off. Thank you SO much for reading Cane's story a bazillion times, sending such detailed notes, reading my rambling stream of consciousness e-mails, and being a blessing above and beyond. Words do not exist to express my gratitude, so I'll just say love you, girl!

Trisha Wolfe and Shannon Duffy deserve medals for putting up with my crazy writing schedule, *especially* toward the end where I sent them 7,000-word chunks. For talking me down off ledges and making me laugh so hard my tummy hurt, thank you, thank you, *thank you.*

Cindi Madsen totally saved my butt in the beginning of this story, and it was through talking with her that the Bachelor Auction came to be…so you can thank her for the delicious abs, ladies. And if you completely melted like I did over Cane's lyrics at the end, I must confess that *all* the credit goes to my girl (and uber-awesome writing bud) Caisey Quinn. She took my pretty speech and turned it into pure gold. I owe her a lifetime supply of chocolate because those lyrics are flipping awesome!

Heather Self and Kayleigh from K-Books are quite honestly the best beta readers EVER. They devoured this book, gave me fabulous feedback, and made me do a bazillion happy dances. Girls, thank you for loving Cane as much as I do!! Before I wrote this book, I already had an author crush on Robin Bielman. When she read *Seven Day Fiancé* and said that she loved it, I about fell out of my chair. That author crush is off the charts about now…

I'm convinced Kelly P. Simmon of InkSlinger PR and Debbie Suzuki aren't human. They are angels with huge hearts and AMAZING talent who were sent to guide me along this crazy journey. Kelly, I'm honored to call you my friend, and Debbie, I'm so stinking excited to have you on my team! Mega shout outs to Christine from I*Heart*BigBooks (and I cannot lie…) for the HOTTEST teasers in the history of the world, and to my agent of awesome Pam van Hylckama Vlieg for all the encouragement. So. Much. Love!

Stacy Cantor Abrams and Alycia Tornetta are hands down the best editors an author can ask for. Their notes are phenomenal, the laughs are constant, and their support and belief in *me* is unconditional. They made this story shine, and made me fall even harder for Cane…a feat I didn't think was possible.

I've been blessed with the most supportive family ever. My husband has helped plot every one of my books, and he always reads the guy parts to make sure they sound like dudes. He takes me out on dates, surprises me with love notes, and does the laundry without asking—proof that real romance exists! My daughters scream from the rooftops that their mama's a writer (and they have crazy loud voices, y'all), and are totally understanding when homeschool time goes wonky due to deadlines. My mom, dad, and brother hear more about the writing process than they *ever* wanted to yet they never fail to ask anyway or to show how proud they are. And my mother-in-law's reign as Number One Cheerleader remains fully intact. *squishes you all*

To every blogger, reviewer, and reader of *Taste the Heat*, a gigantic tackle hug. Your Jason crushes and "Holy Fireman" tweets made me giggle and grin like a loon, and I hope Cane lived up to your expectations. Double tackle hugs go out to The Autumn Review, Harlequin Junkie, Mostly YA Book Obsessed, Starbucks and Book Obsession, Lovin' Los Libros,

Imperfect Women, All Romance Reviews, Jenna Does Books, Book Loving Mom, Stuck in Books, Tangled Up in Books, Always YA at Heart, A Bookish Escape, Dazzled by Books, The Fictionators, Meredith and Jennifer's Musings, K-Books, i*Heart*BigBooks, Library of a Book Witch, Pandora's Books, Crystal in Bookland, Tsk Tsk What to Read, and Just a Booklover for going above and beyond. You made my adult romance debut so fantastic.

And no list of acknowledgements would be complete without a teary-eyed, mushy, and totally sentimental thank-you to my Flirt Squad. Our daily swoons over yummy men, heartfelt chats about life, and giggles over random oddities mean the *world* to me. No other author is as blessed as I am. I love each and every one of your faces, and I can't thank you enough. You inspire me to keep pushing, to keep going, and I love you for it!

About the Author

Rachel Harris grew up in New Orleans, watching soap operas with her grandmother and staying up late sneak-reading her mama's romance novels. Today she still stays up late reading romances, only now she does so openly.

A Cajun cowgirl now living in Houston, she firmly believes life's problems can be solved with a hot, sugar-coated beignet or a thick slice of king cake, and that screaming at strangers for cheap, plastic beads is acceptable behavior in certain situations.

She homeschools her two beautiful girls and watches countless hours of Food Network and reality television with her amazing husband. She writes young adult, new adult, and adult Fun, Flirty Escapes, and LOVES talking with readers! Visit her at www.rachelharriswrites.com.

Find your Bliss with these great releases...

HER SECRET, HIS SURPRISE
a novel by Paula Altenburg

Since being disowned by her strict father, Cass Stone has spent her adulthood trying to prove him wrong. Not even an incredible and mysterious one night stand that leaves her a single mom can trip her up...until the father of her baby stumbles back into her life, as sexy and unreliable as ever. Logan Alexander hasn't forgotten the night he spent with Cass two years ago, but he never expects to end up undercover as her assistant. His job saves lives and he can't afford complications. It's difficult enough to maintain his cover as a carefree wanderer when he realizes his attraction to Cass hasn't faded...and then he meets Cass's daughter.

MAKING WAVES
a Perfect Kisses novella by Ophelia London

When journalist Justine Simms learns the notoriously reclusive pro-surfer Chase Ryder is coming out of retirement for a competition, she knows she's found the perfect exclusive to save her career. Of course, *then* she learns he's the gorgeous, secretly nerdy guy who broke her heart. Will Davenport—aka Chase Ryder—doesn't do interviews. That is, until the still-heartbroken Justine blackmails him into giving her an exclusive. But despite their smoldering attraction, nothing has changed since he had to leave her the first time.

TAMING THE COUNTRY STAR
a Hometown Heroes novella by Margo Bond Collins

Country star Cole Grayson is in town, and Kylie Andrews is less than thrilled. As if months of changing the radio station and tearing down his posters weren't bad enough, now she has to deal with a town of fans swarming toward the man who deceived her the year before. Cole is on a mission. After writing a song just for her, he sets off for her hometown to prove he's not the player she thinks he is.

LOVE FOR BEGINNERS
an Under the Hood novella by Sally Clements

Mechanic Melody Swan is looking for a man who can share her hopes and dreams, but she swore she would never lose herself to passion. When sexy Heath Starr agrees to temporarily sub in the Under the Hood garage for his sister, Mel sees the perfect opportunity to enjoy being with a man without becoming attached. Heath came to Meadowsweet to photograph nature, not find a hookup, especially since his last relationship ended in disaster. When the two find themselves isolated in a rustic cabin, they could both break their promises if they aren't careful…

WILD ABOUT HER WINGMAN
a Secret Wishes novel by Robin Bielman

Erin Watters is her small town's resident wild child—she doesn't do boring, and after having her heart annihilated, she definitely doesn't do relationships. Her friends have other ideas, though, and when they throw down a matchmaking challenge, impulsive Erin can't ignore it. Even when the annoyingly hot Troy Strieber accepts the matchmaker role…Soon what started as an innocent game of matchmaking has them both thinking about the person right under their nose.

Made in the USA
Monee, IL
14 February 2022